PECK FINCH
and the
FOOL

A Peck Finch Novel

Jerome Mark Antil

Copyright © Jerome Mark Antil 2023

ISBN: 979-8-9886448-1-1
(Paperback Edition)

Library of Congress Control Number:

Heartfelt Thanks To:

My Pamela and Marty Bays

LITTLE YORK BOOKS
New York · NY · Dallas · TX

Special thanks to the first lady of New Orleans,

Mayor LaToya Cantrell

Chapter 1

"*Madame*, your bags have been cleared. Welcome to Paris—enjoy your stay," the customs official said.

As Elizabeth began to leave the Charles De Gaulle Airport terminal, she was reading a directional sign for the front entrance when a well-dressed man with black hair and dark sunglasses looked up from a photo he was holding. He nodded for a woman to approach Elizabeth. He put the photo in his pocket. The woman, with outstretched arms, said hello and hugged Elizabeth, kissing both cheeks as if Elizabeth knew her or was expecting her.

"You're here at last, *Madame*," the man said. "Such a long journey. Welcome to Paris."

"Thank you, *Monsieur*."

"*Madame* are you a Victor Hugo fan?" the man asked.

"*Les Miserables*, oh *mais oui, Monsieur*."

The man handed Elizabeth a hardcover book.

"Our welcome gift to Paris, *Madame*—a copy of Hugo's famous *Hunchback of Notre Dame,* fresh from the airport giftshop."

"Thank you so much. I'll treasure it," Elizabeth said.

We've come to give you a lift," the man said.

Elizabeth smiled and stepped outside with them. The man touched a key fob and the side door of a black van with heavily tinted windows slid open. Elizabeth and the woman climbed in the back and the door closed.

"How thoughtful," Elizabeth said. "Does the hotel welcome everyone like this?"

The man climbed into the driver's seat, started the van, drove to the end of the parking concourse, pulled over, and put it in park. He turned around in his seat and with gloved hands pointed a .45 semi-automatic pistol at Elizabeth.

"No one can see you in here, *Madame*," he said.

Elizabeth saw a photograph sticking out of his pocket.

"That picture—that's a picture of me," Elizabeth said.

"No one can hear you, *Madame*," the man said.

"*Pourquoi as-tu cette photo de moi?*" Elizabeth asked. ("Why do you have that picture of me?")

"*Coopérez et vous ne serez pas blessé.*" ("Cooperate and you will not get hurt.")

"*Qui es-tu? J'ai peu d'argent. Qu'est-ce que tu veux?*" Elizabeth asked. ("Who are you? I have little money. What is it you want?")

The man held out handcuffs for the girl beside Elizabeth.

"*Mettez-les sur elle,*" he said. ("Put these on her.")

"How do I—?" the woman asked.

"*Découvrez-le, mais dépêchez-vous, faites-le! Mettez-les sur elle.*" ("Figure it out, but hurry—do it! Get them on her.")

"*Pourquoi me fais-tu ça? je ne suis personne,*" Elizabeth asked. ("Why are you doing this to me? I'm nobody.")

The man grabbed Elizabeth's purse, took out her iPhone and bent it in half. He put it back in the purse, opened the passenger side window and tossed the purse out and into a curbside sewer drain grate.

"*Vous pouvez garder le livre, Madame,*" the man said. ("You may keep the book, *Madame*.")

The man handed a roll of tape and large, black-lensed sunglasses to the girl.

"*Scotchez ses yeux et mettez-les sur elle,*" he said. ("Tape her eyes and put these on her.")

"*Madame, enlève les lunettes avant que nous arrivions là où nous allons et tu vas mourir.*" ("Miss, remove the glasses before we get to where we are going and you will die.")

The man turned around in his driver's seat and drove off.

After nearly an hour in silence, the van came to a full stop, and the driver stepped out to open the side door. The woman sitting next to Elizabeth leaned over and whispered. "They have somebody and will kill him if you resist—shhh!—don't talk, they can hear everything."

It was in New Orleans, twenty-four hours and four thousand, seven hundred and ninety-two miles from Paris, when the nightmare Elizabeth found herself in was about to turn Peck Finch's world upside down. As he often did, he was kneeling in a pew at Cathedral-Basilica, praying. The chancel was his favorite sanctum for self-reflection. He was unaware of what had happened to Elizabeth, but he was distracted. Elizabeth was his first love, and she had moved from Baton Rouge to Paris the morning before. He was nostalgic. The pews were dark, save for a waning daylight illuminating ceiling height, stained glass windows behind the altar. A dusty, golden fog appeared to float out from backlighting of statues of saints including Saint Louis—King Louis IX of France. An imposing cathedra (bishop's seat) was ready in the shadows. A dimly lit lamp hung over the center of the confessional, behind which the priest sat. Father McBride was hearing confessions unusually late that day. Peck had finished his confession and accepted his penance.

"I missed you last week, Peck. I look forward to our chats on your sojourns," Father McBride said.

"I've been in Baton Rouge with a frien', helping her pack, Father. She moved to Paris yesterday."

"Is that why I didn't see you on First Friday—"

"No, Father."

"Are things peaceful in your world, my son?"

"Father, I had to be in court with Lily Cup on First Friday. Then I went to Baton Rouge and packed boxes all week. I called Baitman Alex to go see Mammas and tell her I'd be coming this week instead. I'm going up in the morning."

"Peck, such a colorful array of friends. Do tell your Mammas that I remember her and your grand-mere every morning when I say my Mass."

"I'll be sure to tell her, Father. She'll like that."

"Will you be joining the revelry, Peck?"

"What revelry, Father?"

"It's Bastille Day—an important day for the French—a time for celebration of the history and heritage of St. Louis Cathedral-Basilica, God's house built by and dedicated to the King of France."

"I wasn't planning on it. When I get home I'll see if my frien' Gabe is going to celebrate. I had a long week packing boxes—just drove in from Baton Rouge for confession."

"I must have your opinion of my costume," Father McBride said.

They stepped from the confessional booth. Father McBride's face, ears, and neck were painted white, accentuated with exaggerated black drawn on eyebrows, freckles, and dimples. His striped knit cap of gray and black came to a point. An ivory satin jumpsuit decorated with French vineyard's soft blues, greens, and the browns of leaves and stems. As if his head were on a large, round serving platter, two enormous wafers of heavily starched, white linen were coiled, separated by a hard, candylike ribbon around his collar, circling his neck like a pleated doily.

"Are you a clown, Father?"

"I'm certain there are those who think so, Peck, but not tonight. Tonight, I'm a *mime*—and a mime can't speak or utter a sound. Gestures and expressions are my language tonight. It'll be heaven not having to speak—to remain mum through the entire party."

"I like it, Father McBride. You'll win a prize for sure. When's it start?"

"I'm certain it's already begun, but for me it'll start the minute I step from this church. Which reminds me. I have a favor to ask."

"Of course, Father."

"I'll be leaving through the rectory, and I know you light candles on your way out. Before you leave, Peck, can you be certain you're the last one out?"

"Ah *oui*."

"And would you give an extra nudge on the door when closing it? Listen for the clicking sound. It's self-locking and that will insure it locks."

"Ah *oui*."

"New Orleans festivals do inspire mischief."

"You can count on me, Father."

Father McBride walked to the altar, genuflected, bowed his head, made the sign of the cross, and left the building with an emphatic clunking of the rectory door behind him.

With the night a reality and the rectory lights turned off, the church was now in total darkness save a symphony of votive candles flickering in stair-steps of colorful glass cups, every dancing flame a ballet that kept a remembrance prayer alive—perhaps a sickness or the repose of a soul. Peck lighted two candles and tucked a twenty into the poor box and then felt heavy breathing behind him—an inhaling and exhaling on his neck. He turned to see a thin, masked man in a voodoo costume in full regalia—a tall and tattered top hat, a tuxedo waistcoat with tails, a skeletal mask with heavily blackened eyes, a nose cavity, and a row of top teeth with one missing. The breather's bottom lip and chin were exposed and painted with black lipstick.

The voodoo man stood uncomfortably close. His arm was coiled by a long rubber snake and a long string of enormous wooden Rosary beads was in his other hand. His arms cradled a wooden case. He pointed a warning finger and gave a poke on Peck's shoulder. There was a threatening continence in his demeaner. His eyes were hiding like cowards behind dark, masked eyeholes. The voodoo man wore oversize black boots open at the top with untied laces that promiscuously dragged on the floor.

Peck studied the long wooden case in the man's arms, and wondered why the voodoo man wasn't carrying it by its handle. He smiled before turning his back on the voodoo man to face the candles. Making the turnabout was a statement that he was paying the interrupter of his votive ceremony no mind. When

Peck left the cathedral, he held the door for voodoo man and pushed on the door until he heard the click as Father McBride had asked. The voodoo man followed Peck from the church to his pickup in the parking lot while he chanted in a heavy French accent:

> *"I'm not the one who's so far away, Monsieur,*
> *When I feel the snake bite enter my veins*
> *Never did I wanna be here again, Monsieur,*
> *And I don't remember why I came."*

Peck turned to put an end to this Bastille Day experience.

"It's a nice costume, frien'," Peck said. "Have a good time tonight."

Peck pointed up at the sky. "It's lookin' like lightning up there—maybe an electrical storm. Be careful, mister," Peck said. "Good night."

As he pulled the door of his pickup open, the voodoo man pointed a threatening finger from his fingerless glove and stepped closer to Peck's truck.

> *"Candles raise my desire, Monsieur,*
> *Why I'm so far away*
> *No more meaning to my life, Monsieur,*
> *No more reason to stay."*

"*Monsieur*," Peck said. *"Tu vas t'amuser ce soir dans le quartier—c'est le jour de la Bastille—j'aime ton costume."* ("*Monsieur*, you go have fun tonight in the Quarter—it's Bastille Day—I like your costume.")

Peck turned to board his pickup.

The voodoo man spun around sharply, springing his upper body into a forward lunge like a child's Jack-in-the-Box. Peck turned to watch. He looked into Peck's eyes, and in a tone that screeched like fingernails on a chalkboard, he made a threat.

"If you want her alive, *Monsieur*, you will listen ...."

Peck jolted.

"Want to see her again, oh you sinner from the confessional, you will listen."

Peck froze. He had learned in his early youth of being abused that staring trouble in the face and listening could serve him better than blurting out anything from fear. He had lived in swamps. He knew the danger of showing fear. His silence signaled that he was listening. After the voodoo man's eyes showed a first victory, Peck spoke.

"Who?" Peck asked.

The voodoo man's lower lip sneered, and he wagged his forefinger while uttering an exaggerated *"tsk-tsk,"* implying he'd never tell Peck who was kidnapped.

"Her life is your penance, *Monsieur*," the voodoo man said.

The voodoo man continued:

"I'm not the one who's far away, Monsieur,
When I feel the snake bite enter my veins."

Peck sensed the mention of *"far away"* meant Paris. The mention of *"her"* meant Elizabeth, his lover and friend who had flown to Paris the day before.

Having survived being locked under porches with snakes at the age of four, Peck understood prey and predator. He knew better than to show the predator any sign of fear that could be turned against him. He knew better than to mention Elizabeth's name—or to mention Paris or anything that might be a window to his vulnerabilities as prey. Peck had to somehow reverse the tide and become the predator. He spoke as if only mildly interested.

"Qu'avez-vous fait d'elle?" Peck asked. ("What have you done with her?")

"Votre français est très bon, Monsieur, il vous servira bien pour la tâche à accomplir," Voodoo man said. ("Your French is very good, *Monsieur*, it will serve you well for the task at hand.")

The voodoo man lifted the wooden box by the handle and set it in the bed of Peck's pickup. In full control of his emotions, Peck dialed number 4 on his iPhone. For security he never put names in his phone contacts—only codes he memorized. Elizabeth was number 4. The call went to an incessant busy signal, as though her phone was disconnected.

"Tell me what you want," Peck said.

Voodoo man pointed at the wooden box in the bed of the pickup and with threatening fingers pointed at Peck's eyes.

"Text my phone," voodoo man said.

"What?"

"Do it now."

Peck recognized the man's cell phone as a throw-away.

"Why?" he asked.

"No discussion, *Monsieur*. You will text this phone."

Peck relented. The voodoo man gave him the number and Peck texted it, thus exposing his presence.

With a 'gotcha' sneer in his voice, voodoo man chanted.

"Freezin' feelin'
Breathe in, breathe in, Monsieur,
I'm comin' back again."

Peck bit his tongue, kept silent, and studied the voodoo man making his departure after tripping on his bootlaces, losing his balance, stumbling backward and falling. Picking himself up, the voodoo man sneered while looking at blood on his lower palm from hitting the pavement. He scowled and disappeared through bushes in the direction of sounds of French Quarter revelers. Peck's mind frothed. He jumped in his pickup. His tires screeched under the cotton balls of storm clouds cloaked by muffled lightning flashes.

A local would never drive the Quarter during festivals, but coming from Cathedral-Basilica on Chartres Street at Jackson Square, Peck had little option. He watched for the voodoo man. The crowd was peppered with the same costume. Traffic stalled behind a car hoping to park. Finding street parking in the city of festivals was always difficult. Spaces don't exist until morning, and morning rarely yawns in *Vieux Carrè* before the revelers do, vomiting or pissing in toilets, first opening their eyes to squint through bathroom windows.

In the French Quarter it was masked jubilation everywhere—*noise*—often with a drum thumping at its core. Costumed jaywalkers passed Peck's pickup with expressions of actually getting somewhere, searching for the magic of New Orleans they'd seen in movies. Peck inched toward jazz sounds. *Tuba Skinny* was performing on a corner ahead. He cracked a window and managed a smile at their ragtime. He held two tens out his window. The washboard player took them with a wink and a smile and put them in a tip can.

After passing them, Peck's face morphed into a stare. The night wasn't his usual venue of tracking and investigations. That night was worse. There was no *tell* on his face. It was blanker than faces on the patients at the Carencro hospice who'd stare at the alligator swamp from the hospice's lawn Peck once mowed when he was ten. Peck needed Charlie, political science graduate with a PhD and heir to his daddy's bar, the Blue Note. Charlie was smart. He could cut through issues with incisive candor while pouring a jigger of scotch without spilling a drop. Peck needed Charlie's blade. As a bartender Charlie would entertain and play-act authentic Acadiana persona with the best of them, exaggerate a Cajun French *patois* as he'd slide saucers of crawfish tails to guests at the bar, and getting applause when the saucer stopped in front of its intended patron.

If Peck walked in, he'd put on a show, knowing his friend grew up barefoot, pole-steering a pirogue at six—was dog collared and locked under a porch next to a swamp until he was eight—bound and dragged behind a boat as gator bait until he ran away at nine—and could dish a Cajun patois so thick it would make tourist think they were in another country.

Peck pulled to the curb on Frenchman Street and switched his lights off. A man in a tuxedo walked by carrying a bass fiddle, a burning cigar in his mouth, and a white carnation in his lapel. Peck watched him disappear into the night. He turned in his seat and looked through the rear window.

In the bed of the truck lay the long, V-shaped, wooden crate. It looked handmade and heavily varnished. It glowed a golden halo under a streetlamp that dripped with clinging, beaded necklaces from forgotten memories of parades gone by. There was a *presence* about the crate. It made a statement. It was majestic—as if anointed in some way. The corners were fashioned of finely sanded, dovetail joints. It was an oblong triangle pyramid with a twelve-inch base, and its sides tilted inward up to a narrow five-inch top with a row of evenly placed stainless steel hasps and latches. The crate was bound by antiqued metal straps wrapping it. In the latches were padlocks locking secrets inside. Brass nail heads glowed under the streetlamp. A double thick, heavy leather handle rested on top. Peck knew better than to leave temptation in the bed of his pickup. He lifted his iPhone and touched the code number for Charlie's Blue Note.

Blue Note," Charlie answered.

"What's shakin', frien'?" Peck asked.

"Same old 'ting, new day, where y'at, bébé?"

"I'm on Frenchman Street … thinking."

"Are you okay?"

"I need an ear, frien'."

"You've always got you an ear here, you know that."

"I know."

"Been a while since I've seen you," Charlie said.

"Been up bayou."

"Baton Rouge?" Charlie asked.

"Packing boxes."

"Sounds like you got you an honest gig, eh, bébé?"

"Ah *oui*. Baton Rouge to Paris."

"Is that Elizabeth pretty girl with you?"

"She left yesterday."

"For Paris?"

"Ah *oui*."

"You coming in, bébé, or you going to sit there all night jawing at me and howling at the moon?"

"*Il n'y a pas de lune ce soir, Charlie ...*," ("Ain't no moon tonight, Charlie ....")

"Don't be wasting the French on me, bébé. Is it raining?" Charlie asked.

"Electric storms, looks like, frien'," Peck said. "No rain."

"Dance party's in here, bébé—come pass a good time," Charlie said. "Plenty electricity in here."

"You got a place I can hide something, frien'?"

"Depends what're you hiding?"

"Getting complicated—up to my ass in gators, it seems."

"You've been there before, bébé."

"Not like this, I'm thinking."

"Sounds like you can't talk, bébé—or don't want to."

"Something like that—not from here."

"Is what you've got to hide legal?"

"I don't know."

"Bring it in. Least I asked."

Peck stepped out and locked the pickup. He looked to the sky. He'd often imagine his mamma's face in the moon and she would give him advice. He stared at the crate, as if he was imprinting everything that happened to him that evening in his brain as goslings imprint a mother goose's face.

He picked up the crate and made his way through the velvet sound of a lonely alto sax echoing off brick walls of the dimly lit alley. The band was tuning-up. Another night was climbing out of bed and scratching its balls in the Big Easy. He got to the door, stepped in just as a bass joined the sax with a monotony of scales. Charlie, behind the bar, toweled a rinsed tumbler. Peck nodded. Charlie pointed toward the back room.

"Tell Momma to lock it in a closet."

Peck came from the kitchen and Charlie flagged him over.

"That's an important looking crate, bébé."

"I think they've got Elizabeth, Charlie."

"Good—lucky jazz bistro in Paris—she's a great chef."

"No, frien'—somebody's been kidnapped and I think they got Elizabeth."

"Who would do that sort of thing, bébé?"

"I don't know."

"You're serious aren't you, Peck?"

"I think they got her—dead serious, frien'."

"Did they get her in Baton Rouge—the mob?"

"In Paris."

"You're here, she's there. I don't get it. What do you mean they've got her, Peck? How do you know it's her?"

"I always go to Mass and Confession before I drive up to see Mammas on her houseboat—"

"Peck, we still talking about Elizabeth?"

"Get some fishing in on Diversion Canal and Amite River. That's when I always tell Mammas a book I'm reading, maybe crack some crab and suck a few tails with my frien' Baitman Alex."

"You're in shock, my friend," Charlie said. He handed Peck a shot of tequila. "Throw this back, bébé."

Peck did. He set the empty jigger on the bar.

"I just came from Confession."

Charlie picked up his iPhone and looked at the calendar.

"Bébé, you do that on First Friday. I could swear you do confession on First Friday."

"Ah *oui*."

"First Friday was last week, Peck."

"Last Friday I had to be in court with Lily Cup on a case I was working, so I did Mass and Confession today instead. I was going to drive to Mammas tomorrow."

"Is this what that box Momma locked in the closet is all about, Peck?"

"Ah *oui*."

"Have you called the police?" Charlie asked.

"Not until I talked with you, Charlie. I wanted to hear what you think, first."

"Tell me everything. How'd you wind up with the box? Tell me about Elizabeth—tell me the who and the why."

"The basilica was dark, Charlie, empty at Mass."

"It's Bastille Day, bébé. People are drinking, partying. They're not praying."

"After Confession, like always, I was folding some money in the poor box before I lighted the candles, one for my grand-mère and one for ole Gabe when he comes up behind me, scaring the daylights outta' me."

"Gabe came up from behind?"

"No. A guy in a voodoo costume carrying the box your momma just locked in the closet. He was holding it with both arms, holding it like it was the Holy Grail You know what the Holy Grail is, Charlie?"

"I know the Holy Grail, my friend."

"The voodoo man followed me out and set the box in the bed of my truck. Never asked me. He said if I ever wanted to see her alive, I'd listen."

"Some dude just tells you he has Elizabeth, threatens you with an *or else*, and then leaves a box in your pickup?" Charlie asked.

"He never said her name."

"Who'd he say he grabbed?"

"He just said, '*her*'—"

"Her?"

"But he was dead serious, I watched his eyes."

"You couldn't chance trying something," Charlie said.

"Ah *oui*."

"This is not sounding too good."

"Not so good."

"At least you know she's alive," Charlie said.

"Ah *oui*."

"Did he tell you why he left the box in your truck?"

"He said I'd be hearing from someone."

"You haven't called the police—you didn't call Larry. Think, Peck. You're rattled, bébé. Have you told anyone?"

"Just you. I'm scared, Charlie."

"You're never scared, bébé."

"I don't know if I'd go that far, frien'."

"My advice is to tell nobody—maybe only tell Gabe."

"Hanh?"

"Peck, you're a tracker. I remember you telling me that in tracking, sometimes it's best to make them come to you."

"Dass' for true," Peck said.

"I think this is that time, bébé. Maybe just wait and see."

"I think you're right, frien'."

They shook hands.

"You're at the Blue Note, bébé. Welcome home. Tonight will be about clearing your head. Can you tell by the look of things how important we are now?"

"Charlie's Blue Note, is my favorite place, frien'—it's always important to me. Are you saying it's more important than before? What happened, Charlie—you paint the place? I saw crawfish in the kitchen. Yum. I know that's new."

"Our mayor—" Charlie started.

"Mayor Cantrell—love her," Peck said. "Tough, but tells it like it is."

"Everybody loves LaToya, bébé. Don't you know the mayor of this city of the world walked right up the middle of the street all the way from Jackson Square right through the Quarter with none other than the president of France himself—"

"Are you funnin' me, Charlie? Our mayor walked all this way with the president of France?"

"Walked through the Quarter like it was in their way. All the way here to Frenchman Street to listen to jazz. They heard the prettiest jazz here at the Blue Note. They sat on those stools."

"Are you telling me a president—?"

"President Emmanuel Macron of France—in person— right here at Charlie's."

"Mayor LaToya surely brought the man here, and ain't we something now?" Charlie asked, proudly puffing out his chest.

"On dirait un palais, mon frère. Je suis impressionné."
("It feels like a palace, frien'. I'm impressed.")

"My daddy would be proud," Charlie said.

"He's looking down, Charlie."

"Bébé, was Elizabeth in Baton Rouge when you saw her last?"

"Charlie, I thought you said I should clear my head?"

"I know, I know, but this has a way of grating—"

"It was at Louis Armstrong International last time I saw her. She boarded a plane yesterday morning with a big smile, and I'm pretty sure she slept all the way to Paris."

"And now kidnapped, unless that bastard was pulling one on you. But with that box, I'm thinking he's for real, Peck."

"Ah *oui*."

"Doesn't smell good, Peck. We need Larry in on this."

"I'm shakin' too much to think, frien'. I'll call Larry when I get my head straight."

"That weasel rat snake," Charlie said.

"She was going to live in a hotel until she found a place."

"Bébé, you need to get your head right. You're no good to anyone in a funk," Charlie said.

"Ah *oui*."

"You need to put Elizabeth, the night, and that box out of your head, bébé. You need to get drunk, dance—get lucky in this famous place. Welcome back."

"They're out of my mind, frien', for now anyway, like a casted net at the bottom and forgotten about until I'm hungry."

"Mine too. What can I get you?" Charlie asked.

"Anybody here yet?"

"Band's just warming up. It's early, but Lily Cup's holding a table in the corner for Sasha and Gabe," Charlie said. He pointed. "We're going to be crazy busy tonight with festival junkies, fun and fools. It's Bastille Day."

"I see her."

"Sad eyes on that lady, bébé. Go give your friend some company."

"What happened—she lose a murder case?" Peck asked.

Charlie held out a cold beer.

"Only one way to find out," Charlie said.

Peck pulled a ten-dollar bill from his pocket.

"Your money's no good tonight, bébé," Charlie said. "Put it away. Put everything out of your head."

Peck took the beer and nodded.

Lily Cup, one of Peck's closest friends—a cigar smoking, rye drinking, Harvard Law School, New Orleans criminal attorney who, years ago, drunk on rye the night before a murder trial, maneuvered a young Peck into the Blue Note's ladies' room the night they met. In her midthirties at the time, she seduced the then illiterate nineteen-year-old Cajun French fisher hunk from Carencro. That interlude, and the fact Peck was the best tracker she had met in all her years of practicing law, bonded them and they've mentored each other since—Lily Cup by pushing Peck into literacy, then to night school at Tulane , and Peck, a friend with benefits, the best tracker NOLA law had ever seen, did investigations for her murder trials and for her cop boyfriend and criminal detective, Larry. Peck and Lily Cup had not been intimate since she hooked up with Larry, her "hot chocolate"— the tall, twenty-year unrequited love sweetheart, Creole high school basketball star Lieutenant Larry Gaines, Chief Detective.

Peck walked to her table.

She looked up.

"Beans and rice, cher?" Peck asked.

"Wanna' dance?" Lily Cup asked.

No music was playing.

"When the band starts, I surely will," Peck said.

"I need arms around me."

Peck set his beer on the table and extended his hand. Lily Cup cracked a broken smile. The saxophone player heard her plea, caught her eye, and winked. She rested a cigar in the ashtray, threw back the remains of a jigger of rye and stood in black satin tights and black and silver threaded cashmere top. A foggy sax vibrated from nowhere and muscle memory melted two bodies together like butter with steamed corn. The soft sax moaned a rift so blue that tears made sparkles in Lily Cup's eyes. She buried her face in his neck and they turned a sway in a slow, mindless motion, owning velvet sounds of lost dreams in breezes of loneliness. A brush gently sanded a snare. Peck knew the moment at hand called for him to keep his mouth shut. They danced—bodies moving as one, his arms wrapped around her, keeping her safe.

"You miss Millie?" Lily Cup whispered.

Peck turned them to a rift on the bass and back, upright.

"What made you think of Millie, cher?"

"Do you miss her?"

"When I think of her, I do. I try not to think of her."

"Why'd you two break up?"

"You know why."

"Did you stop loving her, Peck—her you? Remind me."

"I conked them two. You know why, cher."

Lily Cup looked up at Peck.

"They were sex-slavers. You killed bad guys."

"I know, but—"

"Are you saying that's what broke you up?"

"Only three people know I conked 'em, cher."

"So?"

"No way I could tell Millie I did it—you know, killed somebody and not telling her it wouldn't be right waking up next to her knowing I'd be hiding her from a lie like what kind of man I really am."

"I can't believe I'm hearing this."

"What, cher?"

"I need a drink."

Lily Cup stopped dancing and went to the table and poured a jigger of rye. She threw it back and poured another. Peck sat down.

"You're thinking if Millie knew you killed them and got away with it, and you two ever got in a fight—with no statute of limitations on murder, that she might ..."

"I wasn't thinking that, cher, but two big words—
might, could."

Lily Cup lighted her cigar.

"Millie's not the type," Lily Cup said.

"How so?"

"She worshipped you."

Lily Cup jerked her head up and looked him in the eyes.

"Wait—" Lily Cup said.

"What?"

"You said three people knew."

"Ah *oui*," Peck said.

"Three people don't know, Peck. Only me and Larry. Chris the coroner doesn't know and you didn't tell Gabe. So that makes Larry, me, and we've got you covered. *Cause of Death* papers fixed at the morgue, dated and stamped off as closed cases and in *closed case* dead files a year ago."

"You're the best, cher."

Lily Cup sensed his holding back.

"Something you're not telling me, Peck?"

Peck had confessed the murders a year ago to Father McBride on a First Friday confession. But he remembered Charlie's advice to get everything out of his head for the night, so he didn't respond to Lily Cup. He asked her if she wanted to dance some more.

Lily Cup stood up and embraced Peck.

"Who's three, Peck? Who else knows?"

Peck ignored her.

Peck turned her to a piano rift.

Lily Cup shook her head, reached around him and pulled him closer, burying her face into his neck.

"Just dance," she whispered.

"Forget me, cher. Let's talk about you."

Lily Cup didn't respond.

"I know you pretty good, I'll say. Something you're not telling me," Peck said.

No response.

"You say we've got no secrets," Peck said.

No response.

Peck lifted her chin with his finger.

"Cher, you just grabbed my ass …"

Lily Cup rolled her eyes. "You complaining?"

"Larry's your man. Something's on your mind, that's for dang sure, the way you just squeezed my ass. I'm here for you, cher."

"Larry's going back to his wife," Lily Cup replied. "For the kids."

Peck didn't respond.

He lowered his cheek to hers, they closed their eyes and moved to the music as people stepped around them to get to tables.

"I love the man, but kids need a daddy," Lily Cup said.

"Ah *oui*," Peck said.

"A conundrum," Lily Cup said.

"Is it a done thing?"

"It has to be."

"Is it over—you two even, like, doing it?"

"It's the same with you and Millie. You didn't want to live a lie. Same here with Larry and me, Peck. He doesn't want to live a lie with his boys."

"Larry's a good man. You're a good woman. I see why it has to be over."

"I love that man more than I've ever loved anybody—and I think his wife's a 'C' the way she disrespects the hours his career requires. But those two beautiful black boys here in the murder capital of the hemisphere need a daddy. They need their own daddy—at home."

"Larry never said anything to me, cher."

"You've been in Baton Rouge while all this went down."

"Cher?" Peck asked.

"Uh huh?"

"Can I bed you?"

Lily Cup looked him in the eyes and smirked.

"I don't need a *mercy* booty call, Peck."

"It's been a long time, cher …."

Lily Cup smiled and nodded.

Peck whispered in her ear.

"I know you broke it off with your man—he's my good frien'—but you are split and I've got a lot on my mind and I know you've got a lot on your plate. I thought maybe if we got together, you know …."

"Only if you promise we turn the phones off—keep them off until morning."

"Anything, cher."

Lily Cup reached around Peck and took the phone from his back pocket and turned it off. Her left hand reached and slid the phone back into the pocket while her right hand gripped his package, marking her territory.

"You're mine tonight."

"My phone's been off for hours," Lily Cup added. She took his arm and walked him like royalty to the door.

"Tomorrow, cher, remind me of *conundrum*?"

"Conundrum? Why?"

"I want to look it up."

Lily Cup caught Charlie's eye.

"Charlie, put a *Reserved* plaque on our table?"

"Will do. You two have you a good time, that's for sure."

"Tell Sasha I'll see her tomorrow—lunch at Antoine's," Lily Cup said.

"Will do."

"Tell her something's come up."

She grinned.

Peck caught Charlie's eye and gave a thumbs up. "Charlie, when Gabe comes in tell him I'll see him for breakfast," he said.

Charlie grinned and winked at Peck.

Chapter 2

Peck stepped from the shower in Lily Cup's guest bathroom just as Lily Cup walked in.

"Aren't you going to sleep in my room?"

"Ah *oui*—but it's a better shower in this room. Been packing, boxing, and driving all day—sweaty—I needed a good shower."

"Leave it running," she said.

She pushed her tights and panties from her hips to the floor and stepped out. With an ankle swipe, she kicked them onto the guest bed. She pulled her sweater over her head and off, unsnapped her bra and tossed them on the bed while Peck stood toweling himself. Lily Cup sneaked a peek at his *William*, smiled and motioned her head toward her bedroom. *William* became the moniker Lily Cup and Sasha used to reference Peck's *waggle* after watching him step out of a bathtub at the Peabody Hotel in Memphis.

"There's a raw bar on my desk—oysters," Lily Cup said.

"Aye-*yi-yi*!" Peck said.

"Don't wait on me. I'll be there in a minute. Go eat."

She pulled the shower door behind her.

In her bedroom, still naked but dry, Peck was sliding his third oyster with cocktail sauce onto his tongue, chasing it down with a shot of tequila as a bare-breasted Lily Cup walked in, a towel draped around her hips.

"You look so good, cher."

"How are the oysters?" Lily Cup asked.

"The best this season," Peck said.

"Commander's Palace. I ran over and got them while you showered. Thought we'd have some fun."

"Cher, it feels like Larry's ghost is in the room."

"His spirit is. It will be until that one day."

"You still love him, cher."

 "I'll always be here for that man."

"He's a good man and good frien'."

"He thinks of you as a brother, Peck. He respects you."

"Is he going to mind, you know—us here—if we?"

"He'd be disappointed if we didn't," Lily Cup said.

"For true?"

"Peck, his and my split has to be real—for his kids. We'll never break up, but we have to split—cut ties."

"I understand, cher."

"If his boys are ever going to make it in today's world, I've got to help him. I've got to be a free woman."

She copped a feel of *William*.

"I can't fake it."

Peck fed Lily Cup oysters. Together they polished off the raw bar. She stepped over to the bed and pulled the comforter and top sheet down.

"Favor, hon?" Lily Cup asked.

"Anything," Peck said.

"Dump the ice in the tub? It'll melt on the desk."

Peck carried the tray to the bathroom. He took the oyster shells and put them in the plastic bag lined waste basket. He tied the bag's top. He emptied the ice in the tub, rinsed the tray and dried it with a face towel.

He turned the bathroom light off and stepped into the bedroom. The desk lamp was still on. Lily Cup was lying on her side, her back to him. Peck went to the other side of the bed and watched her with her praying hands between her cheek and a soft feather pillow, sound asleep. One of the most caring people he knew was worn out. In a sometime man's world of criminal law, she could keep up with the best of them, own the judges or district attorneys, if she needed them. She was a woman in love. But she was a woman with the integrity her daddy taught her about doing the right thing, no matter what sacrifice it cost—no questions asked. Giving a daddy back to two impressionable young boys could save their lives. A father as role model, teacher, mentor, helping them with their choices. Peck knew Lily Cup and Larry taking a break was the right thing to do, regardless of how much it hurt.

Peck stepped to the closet and pulled the door open. On the shelf was a teddy bear wearing a Harvard Law T-shirt. He took it down, stepped over to the bed and nestled it against Lily Cup's chest until her subconscious took her hands from under her cheek and clutched the Teddy as naturally as she might have in her teens. With a sleepy happy smile, she rolled over, snuggling Teddy.

Peck decided to let her sleep. He walked around the bed and sat, staring at the desk lamp. Had Elizabeth really been kidnapped? Was she okay? What was she doing? Could he save her? He stood, went to the desk and scribbled a note about his coming back another night if Lily Cup would have him. He tucked Lily Cup and Teddy in, put the note on the side table, dressed, turned the desk light off and left the house.

Chapter 3

Peck pulled up the drive at the shotgun house. The house lights were off. He unlocked the door, stepped in and switched on kitchen lights. Through Gabe's bedroom door he heard snoring. He went in and put a hand on his friend's shoulder.

"It's me, Captain," Peck said.

Gabe lifted his head from the pillow.

"You tired, ol' man?"

"My brother," Gabe said.

"Aren't you going to the Blue Note tonight, ol' man?"

"Tomorrow night. Sasha came by. She has a dinner meeting—had to beg out of Charlie's tonight."

"Sorry to wake you."

"Waking at my age, son, is a privilege."

"Ha. Wanna talk, Gabe?"

"Put a pot on. I'll splash my face."

Peck went to the kitchen, feeling himself in a mindless daze from the stress of thinking about Elizabeth. He went through the chicory coffee routine like a robot as he had done so many times before, having to walk three miles to mow lawns from age nine to nineteen. He spooned five scoops of chicory in the Mr. Coffee filter cup and dusted it with ground cinnamon. Seven spoons of Splenda *no calory* sweetener into the pot before filling it with cold tap water to dissolve the Splenda. He poured it in and turned the maker on as Gabe passed through the kitchen to the living room and his recliner. Peck followed, clicked his iPhone on and sat down. There were no calls or messages on his phone.

"How've you been, frien'?" Peck asked.

"Missed you, my brother. It's not easy cooking for one, but knowing you were packing up Elizabeth for her Paris adventure warmed my heart, let me smile from time to time, remembering good times me and my army buddies had in Paris back when."

"Elizabeth's full head chef at a new bistro they're opening on the Left Bank."

"I'm happy for her, son."

"Going to run the whole show, Gabe. She worked hard to earn that spot," Peck said.

"She's a good woman, son."

"They're going to have live jazz at her new bistro. She says it'll be sounds coming straight from New Orleans."

"I'd love Paris, one more time. Oh my," Gabe said.

"Maybe we can, Gabe. I got you to Newport for jazz."

"My brother." Gabe smiled. "Tell me what you've been up to, son."

"Just packing."

"Peck, you come home at this hour, you come in my room and wake me and ask if I want to talk. Something's on your mind, my brother. Why're we dancing—to no music, no coffee?"

Peck jumped up, went and got cups of coffee.

"Gabe, I've been packing for Elizabeth."

"If you've got something on your mind, son, spit it out."

"I went to Confession at the Basilica."

"Today?"

"Ah *oui*."

"Is it First Friday already?" Gabe asked.

"First Friday was last week," Peck said.

"You do Confession on First Fridays, son—what's up?"

"Last Friday I had to be in criminal court—Tulane and Broad—with Lily Cup, so I went to Confession today. I'm going to Mammas tomorrow."

"Now it's making sense. Will you be dropping traps?"

"Ah *oui*. I'll call Baitman Alex. He'll toss ten."

"Bring some crab back. I'll make an *etouffee*. How is Mammas?"

"Baitman Alex tells me she's doing good, Gabe. I'll tell her you were asking."

"What's on your mind, son?"

"Gabe, after Confession a dude in a costume followed me to my pickup."

"This is New Orleans—it happens. What costume?"

"A voodoo costume—top hat, skeleton mask with top teeth, only he was carrying a rubber snake and rosary beads."

"It's Bastille Day. They'll be crazies out tonight, son."

"Gabe, he was carrying a long wooden box container with metal straps and padlocks."

"Part of his costume?"

"He put it in the back of my pickup, Gabe."

"The wooden container he was carrying?"

"Ah *oui*."

"Maybe it was a costume prop he was just getting rid of."

"He told me if I ever want to see *her* again, I'd listen."

"Run this by me again?"

"This voodoo man followed me from the Basilica out to the parking lot and he told me if I ever want to see *her*, I'd listen."

"Your voodoo man has a screw loose, is all, son. Was he hammered?"

"Gabe, he had cold dead eyes. He wasn't playing."

Gabe sat up, straightening his recliner.

"Did you say he said *her*? Gabe asked.

"Ah *oui*."

"Didn't use a name or tell you who, he just said, her....?"

"Her," Peck said. "That's all he said."

"So, *her* could be anybody. It could be Sasha, Lily Cup, just about anybody—even somebody he made up."

"Ah *oui*—that's just it, Gabe—I'm not sure who it is, but when he said it, I'm thinking he means Elizabeth."

"When does Elizabeth leave for Paris?" Gabe asked.

"She's in Paris. Got there last night."

"Have you tried calling her?"

"I get a busy signal, like it's disconnected, Gabe."

"Try it now, my brother."

Peck touched contact 4 on his phone. It returned an endless busy signal.

"Nothing," Peck said.

"So, he followed you out of the church?"

"In a voodoo costume. Followed me to the parking lot."

"And you've never seen him before?"

"Never."

"He doesn't say anything, just follows you out?"

"He talked. He had a heavy French accent and was—how you say—chanting like a verse, about snakes and distance and that he didn't want to be there. It was like he was on drugs or something."

"Let me get this right. A man wearing a voodoo costume follows you carrying something important that he's going to wind up putting in your truck?"

"Ah *oui*."

"And he didn't hand it to you to carry for him?"

"*Mais non*." (No.)

"And it's not a gift for you?"

"*Mais non*." (No.)

"He carries it himself—to your pickup?"

"Ah *oui*."

"Padlocks, son? You said padlocks, not padlock?"

"Ah *oui*."

"More than one padlock?"

"Ah *oui*."

"How many?"

"I don't know."

"Padlocks on the same latch, or on different latches?"

"Different latches."

"Then what—?" Gabe asked.

"He told me if I wanted to see *her* again, I better listen."

"He only referred to this person as *her*?" Gabe asked.

"Ah *oui*."

"Anything else?"

"He didn't say her name."

"Anything else, son?"

"That's all, Gabe. Then he disappeared."

"Did you see him go back to the cathedral?"

"No, he went into the French Quarter."

Gabe sipped his coffee.

"What are you thinking, ol' man?"

"You said his accent was a heavy French?"

"Ah *oui,* very heavy French. Almost—how you say—guttural."

"Sounds to me like it could be a 'stage French' accent. Could be a phony masquerading as French."

"Stage French, Gabe?"

"Rehearsed. Maybe he doesn't speak French—like an actor," Gabe said.

Peck played the voodoo man's voice over in his mind.

"Peck, think of your fisher days back in the swamps."

"Hanh?"

"What was the first thing you'd do when you got to a swamp or to a shore of the bayou—before you'd cast your net or climb in your pirogue—first thing you'd do?"

"I'd lean on a cypress tree."

"Why?"

"To be still—not draw attention—watch and listen."

"Watch and listen for what, son?"

"Sounds, Gabe. Movement, things like that. Sounds could be in the grass, on the ground, in weeds, through reeds in the swamp, they could be up on Cypress branches—"

"And from what you saw or listened to, what might you learn?"

"I'd know what's there—where it was and what bait to try."

"Exactly. You'd scope and you'd know—best guess."

"Pretty much, ol' man. Hearing a crawfish snake rustling through grass toward a part of the swamp usually meant crawfish maybe showing their heads coming up for air from the bottom, and good place for snakes to catch them some breakfast crawfish and for me to catch snappers on the bottom already chomping on crawfish down there. If Carrion crows were up high on branches that could be that mashwarohn were scavenging and sending gator or heron bit off fish heads and fish body parts up to float—a good place to cast a net for catfish. Vultures smell death a mile off, Gabe, and it takes a bottom feeder like mashwarohn to float dead fish parts up to the surface."

"My brother, you've fed yourself since you were nine. You never asked for or took a dime for something to eat."

"I traded my catch for eggs and chicory, Captain. I boiled eggs in the coffee pot that nice man, boat builder Marcel LaFleur, let me use, I'd eat two eggs for breakfast before walking barefoot to the hospice to toss my net in the swamp there and to mow their lawns. I carried two eggs for my lunch."

"You're the best fisher around, son. There's a word for what you looked for every time—you remember?"

"Tell me, Gabe."

"*Signs*, my brother."

"Ah *oui*."

"You look for the signs. You study everything. You keep your eyes and ears open. Gives you a better chance of catching everything. You have to think about signs tonight."

"You tell me, Gabe."

"It has to come from you, my brother. Your brain can't help it. It won't rest until you solve this and Elizabeth—if it's her—is safe. This mystery has only begun—but you'll figure it out."

"Peck made the sign of the cross and kissed his thumb. "You think, Gabe?"

"I'm an old man. My mind is in semiretirement—might say in enemy territory. Your brain's still a whir. It's up to you, now."

"I can't figure what the box has to do with it, Gabe."

"I can't either. But there's a reason he left it."

"What's it all saying to you, Gabe?"

"You'll have to find that out on your own, son. I'm thinking you need to talk with Larry—see what he has to say."

Peck blessed himself again and kissed his thumb.

"Gabe, Lily Cup and Larry—how you say—broke up."

"My brother, Lily Cup and Larry will never break up. But it's true they've split to save his two boys. Lily Cup earns a special spot in heaven for that one—him, too."

"Now I know why you earned medals in the army, Gabe. You're a good detective, frien', when it comes to clear thinking, and I thought Charlie was good."

"Charlie's a good mind, son."

"I know, Gabe. He cuts through to the middle of it, and he does that good, but you peel it."

"Layers of skin tell more secrets," Gabe said.

"You're both good, Captain," Peck said.

"What's next, son?"

"Aurelie, I'm thinking."

"Help me. Who is Aurelie, again?"

"Aurelie—at the phone store on Canal Street."

"I remember."

"She's my frien'."

"I see her sometimes at Charlie's, Peck."

"If she can go, I'll take her to Mammas. I have homework to do on this mess. Aurelie knows computers, understands messes."

Gabe sipped coffee and handed his mug to Peck to hold for him so he could stand up without spilling it. He took the mug and walked to his bedroom.

"Grab some sack time, son. I'll have whitefish, potatoes, and onions in a pan when you wake up."

Chapter 4

It was 1:00 a.m. when a pounding rattled the shotgun house door. Peck jumped from bed, and with stealth crept into the kitchen, only to see it was Lieutenant Larry on the stoop, holding a flashlight on his face. Peck smiled, switched the lights on and opened the door.

"You want coffee, Lieutenant?" Peck asked.

"Put some pants on, Peck. Let's go for a ride."

"What's up?"

Larry stood expressionless.

"Is this about Lily Cup, Larry?"

Larry motioned his head toward Peck's bedroom as if telling him to go get some clothes on. Peck went to his room and came back dressed. They stepped out. Peck locked the door.

"Want me to follow you somewhere?" Peck asked.

"We're going to the Blue Note," Larry said.

"Charlie's? What for?" Peck asked.

Frenchman Street was jammed—no parking available. Peck waited. Larry tapped on his window. Peck rolled it down.

"Peck, pull it in the alley and park ten feet from Charlie's door, so folks can get in and out. I'll park behind you and call in your plate that we're both here on an investigation."

Peck closed his window. They parked next to the alley's brick wall and met at the Blue Note's front door.

"Larry, they bombed my truck—on this street— remember? If one goes off in this alley, it'll take both buildings with it."

"Your pickup's safe, Peck—different time, different signs."

"There's that word again," Peck said.

Larry pulled the Blue Note door open and they stepped in.

"What word again?" Larry asked.

"Signs," Peck said.

Larry looked at Charlie.

"Is she here yet?" Larry asked.

A lady in her early forties turned on a barstool.

"Here I am, Lieutenant," she said.

"Lizzie," Larry said. "Peck, meet Lizzie. We call her Locksmith Lizzie. Lizzie, meet my friend, Peck."

"Hi Lizzie," Peck said.

"Hi Peck. Nice to meet you. I've heard good things."

"Let's go in the kitchen," Larry said.

"Did Lily Cup call you, Larry?"

"Charlie called me. I don't know what's going on, but he asked me to cover your back."

Lizzie and Peck shook hands, and the three of them started toward the kitchen. Charlie picked up a small toolbox from behind the bar and handed it to Lizzie. The kitchen had closed at ten o'clock, so Larry felt the wall in the dark for a switch and turned the lights on. He pointed at a stainless steel table, suggesting Lizzie might use it as her worktable. He took a key ring from his pocket and unlocked the closet and pointed to the wooden case standing on its end. He shook his finger to get both Peck's and Lizzie's attention and touched his pursed lips with the finger, signaling them not to talk. He pulled a pad from his pocket, scribbled, and held it up.

"No talking—we might be bugged."

Peck and Lizzie nodded. Larry pointed at the container in the closet. Peck knew Larry could surmise it was the box—but he also knew Larry was fanatical about not missing a single detail. "Never guess or gamble," he would say. "If you stack facts like poker chips, you'll be at the table for your good hands."

"Is this the box?" Larry's note asked.

Peck nodded *yes*.

Larry scribbled and handed a note to Peck and Lizzie.

"I'm going to want to have this thing dusted for prints, so no one touch the container itself—just the handle or padlocks."

He pulled on rubber gloves and lifted it from the closet and set it on the table. Peck and Lizzie waited for a signal. The note came.

"Lizzie, try to open it by only touching the locks. Think you can do that?"

Lizzie took Larry's pad from his hand and wrote, *"These are easy locks to pick—school locker padlocks. No problem."*

Larry offered two sweeping opened palms, inviting her to give it a try. He backed out of the way and stood with Peck.

One by one Lizzie turned the dial back and forth through numbers, feeling for click or *nick* sounds, pausing occasionally as if holding her breath while pushing the lock up and down to open. Peck counted twelve locks as they were being unlocked and removed from a latch of the mysterious wooden crate. Lizzie stood back and let Larry come forward to open it. Lizzie took a wireless bug detector from her tool box and stood waiting for his signal. Larry carefully opened the container lid and lifted the top back to a rest on its hinges. He nodded at Lizzie, signaling her to do her thing. Carefully, meticulously Locksmith Lizzie scoured every inch, every nook and cranny of the mysterious container with her gadget. She shook her head *no* to Larry. There was no bug.

"That's a relief," Larry said. "Well done, Lizzie."

"Thank you, Lieutenant."

"Let's have a look inside," Larry said.

He motioned for Peck to step forward.

"Here's where you come in, Peck. Do your magic."

"Ah *oui*. I understand."

Peck stepped in, leaned over. "Larry, you make the notes?" Peck asked.

"At your service, Boudreaux Clemont. Fire away." Larry had pen and pad in hand.

Like a vacuum brush on carpet fiber, Peck's eyes scoured the inside of the opened wooden box inch by inch, and he started rambling as his eyes caught things.

"There's—looks like gold. Could be picture frames."

"Should they be dusted for prints?" Larry asked.

"I'm thinkin' probably not, Larry. If they do have prints, they could be about anyone's prints—wasting our time. The gold looks like it's on wood, not plated on metal or real gold. I'm thinkin' if they're store-bought they could be loaded with prints from a lot of people."

"Got it."

"There are fourteen frames, and they're four, maybe four and a half, inches apart from each other. Between each frame is white Styrofoam packing material. ..."

"Should we lift one out, see what it is?" Larry asked.

"Could be booby-trapped. Let's leave them in," Peck said. "The inside of the container is lined with blue velvet, perfectly stitched with no curves—only straight lines—like in the saxophone case I saw under the bridge in Providence that night with Sasha. I forget what she called the color."

"Royal blue?" Larry asked.

"*Aye-yi-yi!*" Peck said. "That's it."

"Anything else, Peck?"

"Larry, Lizzie, take a look here at the underside of the top of the box."

"What about it?" Larry asked.

"Two things, I'm thinkin'," Peck said.

Larry gently elbowed Lizzie to pay close attention, hinting the Peck Finch *eye* was about to unmask the big clue of the night.

"Watch this," Larry said.

Peck started. "First thing is—about the underside of this box's top—it's lined with canvas. It's not lined like the other inside parts with velvet. It's been dyed royal blue like the rest, but it's canvas, not velvet."

"You said two things, Peck."

"Get in close," Peck said.

Larry and Lizzie leaned in.

"There're two parts to this box, Larry. Look close at the bottom and you can see the velvet walls inside the container are neatly trimmed and neatly stitched. No edges that aren't sewn in a—how you say—hemmed way like a curtain would be hemmed."

"And?" Larry asked.

"Look at the canvas in the top part of the box, Larry."

"The top. I'm looking. What about it? I see canvas."

"It's not what you can see, Larry. It's what you don't see."

"What don't I see, Peck? I'm lost."

"The top canvas part is not trimmed, Larry. There's not a stitch in it."

"It's not what?"

"It's not trimmed or stitched."

"I don't get it, Peck."

"The bottom of the box is trimmed and sewn. The boxes top's canvas is not trimmed on all four sides means the canvas hasn't been cut. It's been scissor cut but not hemmed."

"Is that important?" Larry asked.

"It means the canvas was turned up and rolled over the space on top of it. Everything that's over the underside of this lid or inside it is covered with one piece of canvas."

"What are you saying? Are you saying the top is hollow?"

"I'm saying there's a secret compartment up there. If you don't want to get something hidden in there wet, Larry, you use canvas. You don't cut it or stitch it, you roll it up like a paper sandwich sack."

"You thinking there might be something hidden in the space between the lid and that lower panel?" Larry asked.

"Not thinking, Larry."

"How sure are you?" Larry asked.

"I pretty much know, Larry."

"Lizzie, let's get someone over here who can open it," Larry said.

"Why take that chance?" Peck asked.

"You have a problem with that, Peck?"

"If we open it, they'll know we've opened it. That could get Elizabeth killed."

"I see your point, Peck."

"I'm already thinking I know what their game is, Larry. Let me catch them?"

"I'm game. Any ideas?"

"They leave a fancy, expensive wood box in a stranger's truck. …"

"I'm listening."

"Maybe it's only a lure," Peck said.

"Could be that," Larry said.

"But what if they're doing the same thing that happened on those cases of the kidnappers we solved—where that lawyer and his wife were kidnapping one of them and blackmailing their mates to steal and rob for them?"

"You think?"

"But bigger this time, Larry, maybe."

"Lizzie," Larry said, "in that criminal case, a lawyer and his wife kidnapped vulnerable people, blindfolded them and hid them out of town in cages to get their spouses or lovers to commit crimes—burglaries—watches, jewelry."

"I'm thinking this is that, but bigger, Larry."

"How's it bigger, Peck?"

"Those kidnappers were local. If he's got Elizabeth, she's in Paris—and he's French."

"That's something I can't seem to get my head around, Peck. Elizabeth being in Paris."

"What do you mean?" Peck asked.

"Who the hell in Paris would know her when she came through customs? Did somebody board the same plane, follow her from Baton Rouge?"

"How would they know what flight she was on? You're right, Larry. Now I'm lost," Peck said.

"Sounds like it's you they want, Peck, not Elizabeth."

"That's what I'm thinking, Larry—kidnap Elizabeth and blackmail me like the jewelry store robbers we caught."

"Sounds like it," Lizzie said.

"If someone in Baton Rouge had access to her phone, they could maybe see her airline ticket information—if they could get into it," Larry said.

"Or if someone knew her flight and told somebody or were—how you say—overheard her talking about it," Peck said.

"We've got a lot to unravel. Hidden secrets we have to find out soon," Larry said.

"Let's set a trap by doing what they say to do," Peck said.

"Undercover. Good possibility, Peck."

"I'm thinking this guy's looking for—how you say—a mule, Larry."

"Drug mule?"

"Like that—some kind of mule."

"I'm listening."

"He speaks with a French accent—maybe lives in Paris, Larry. Maybe he's got a place here, too. But I think he needs a mule to get this box through American and French customs—a mule to Paris. Elizabeth is the bait."

"Smuggler," Larry said.

"A smuggler that won't get caught. If anyone gets caught, it'd be me," Peck said.

"We could take the box back to the parking lot—sit and wait—and if he showed we'd grab him," Larry said. "He wouldn't have time to signal Paris."

"Let's play it out, Larry. Let's watch. Let's not put Elizabeth in more danger. Let's learn what their game is, then we'll catch 'em—how you say—red-handed, both here and in Paris at the same time and save Elizabeth. Think about it, Larry. There has to be a bad guy helping voodoo man on the other end, in Paris."

"I can buy that."

"Good," Peck said.

"Sounds like a plan," Larry said.

"I'll find the voodoo man and tell him. I'll do what he says," Peck said.

"Go slow, Peck. Not too fast."

"Hanh?"

"Give in, but not without a struggle, Peck," Larry said.

"What do you mean, frien'?"

"You've given him no indication you'd do anything for him, right?"

"Right."

"Popping up all of a sudden and saying you're ready to give in, might spook him—scare him away, your turning on a dime like that. It could get Elizabeth killed and the bad guys on the run."

"Good thinking."

"Play it out, Peck. Keep your phone charged and on. See if he messages or calls you.

"I know how to lay a trap, Larry."

"Don't train him, Peck."

"What do you mean?"

"Don't mention Elizabeth's name ever. Use no names."

"Ah *oui*."

"And if he mentions names, including Elizabeth's, don't react—almost like you don't know her."

"Delete your phone contacts so they can't read names."

"No names in my contacts. None in Elizabeth's. Only numbers."

"Perfect. We shouldn't use phones to talk. Yours could be bugged. Stay away from my station, too. They could be Google-tracking your phone."

"Give me a day with Aurelie's computer. I'll text you from her phone."

"Lizzie, lock it up and lock it in the closet."

"Are we dusting it for prints, Lieutenant?" Lizzie asked.

"Won't do any good. Whoever's behind this is too smart to leave prints," Larry said.

"Voodoo man had gloves on, but costume gloves. His fingers were bare, Larry," Peck said.

"You're shitting me," Larry said. "He had bare fingers?"

"Ah *oui*."

"He's careless, Peck. That will be his first mistake. Dust it, Lizzie," Larry said. "Methinks we're dealing with a careless crook—the most dangerous kind of criminal."

Lizzie dusted it and found no prints.

"Our voodoo man just got lucky," Larry said.

He took the box to the closet and locked it in.

"Night, Lieutenant," Lizzie said.

"Night, Lizzie, night Peck."

"Night," Peck said. "Nice to meet you, Lizzie."

"Peck?" Larry asked.

"Ah *oui*?" Peck asked.

"Every time you talk with him, make him prove she's alive," Larry said.

They left Charlie's Blue Note.

Chapter 5

Peck parked on Canal Street. City workers swept leftover debris from the Bastille Day celebration. He picked up the chicory and a Chai tea from the console and walked to the cell phone store, sipping his chicory. In the store he spotted Aurelie on a bench reading the back of a box of earphones.

"Hey, bébé."

Aurelie looked up, smiled, and stood to greet her friend.

"You need a phone, or you here because you miss me?" Peck handed Aurelie her tea.

"I miss my Zydeco dancing frien' from up bayou."

They hugged.

"When do you get a break, bébé?" Peck asked.

"Why? What's up?"

"A frien's been kidnapped."

"Oh my God, Peck, don't kid like that."

"For real. She's been kidnapped."

"Who? Is she okay?"

"I don't know if she's okay, but I have to find her."

"How can I help?" Aurelie asked. "What can I do?"

"I need some, I need—how you say—some research done, looking for things on the computer."

The phone store manager walked by. She was a tall, confident, black woman with shoulder-length hair and a captivating smile.

"It's slow today, Ms. Dillon, can I maybe take the day? I need to do something important."

"That'll be fine, Aurelie. Just tell Joseph you're checking out. Tomorrow's your day off. You'll be here Sunday, right?"

"Yes ma'am, I will."

"Ms. Dillon, I'd like you to meet my friend, Boudreaux Clemont Finch. He and I grew up near each other up bayou. We only met for the first time a year ago. Small world, huh?"

"It certainly is a small world—imagine," Ms. Dillon said.

"Boudreaux and I do Zydeco, Ms. Dillon. Sometimes we dance jazz at Charlie's Blue Note on Frenchman Street."

"I've done a bit of jazz dancing myself—such fun," Ms. Dillon said.

"Boudreaux, meet Ms. Dillon, our store manager and my friend for all the time I've been here."

"Call me Ronda," Ms. Dillon said, shaking Peck's hand. "Very nice meeting you, Boudreaux, dancing man."

Peck and Ms. Dillon shook hands

"You need to meet my frien' Gabe, Ma'am—he's old but he's the dancing man—dass' for true."

"Really? Good dancing has no age on it. It's not easy finding a good dancing man, these days," Ms. Dillon said.

"Nice to meet you, Ronda. Call me Peck."

"Hi, Peck. You two run along and have a great day."

Ms. Dillon stepped away to greet a customer.

Peck and Aurelie climbed in the pickup and sipped their coffee and tea.

"You got your computer, bébé?"

"It's at my apartment."

"Want to go with me to see my Mammas on her houseboat for the weekend—get some fishing in?"

"Where?"

"Mammas's houseboat is on Diversion Canal, near the Amite River. I always tell Mammas about a book I'm reading. We maybe crack some crab and suck a few tails with my frien', Baitman Alex. Want to go with me, bébé? We can do the research there."

"I'd love to go, but only if I can be back tomorrow. It could even be late tomorrow night, but I can't go if I can't get back until, at the very latest Sunday morning, before I have to be at work."

Peck started the engine and they headed to her apartment for her bag and iPad. Within the hour they were on their way to the cozy houseboat on a canal up bayou. Passing Lake Pontchartrain, Peck picked up his iPhone in thought. He touched number 4 (Elizabeth's number) and got a steady busy signal. He touched 7. It rang three times and Audrey, his tarot card reader, answered.

"Are you all right, Peck? For some reason I was thinking of you," Audrey said.

"I need a reading, Ms. Audrey. I need it bad."

"Are you in Baton Rouge?"

"I'll be there in an hour, Ms. Audrey, if you can see your way."

"Come here directly, Peck. I'll clear the morning."

The call ended and Peck set his iPhone in the center console. Aurelie watched the sights as they passed century-old Cypress trees standing guard over the swamps, bayous and shading the bridges of Acadiana—her childhood heritage.

Chapter 6

Aurelie was asleep by the time Peck parked in front of Audrey's.

He gently squeezed her thigh. "Bébé, you want to nap out here—I'll be an hour—or do you want to come in and wait in there?"

"I'll snooze—you go. If I get bored, I'll walk."

Peck went to the door and knocked. Audrey opened it and put arms out for a hug. Peck obliged.

"This morning I couldn't get your face out of my head, Peck, for some reason. Then you called me out of the blue, pray tell, is anything amiss?"

"Audrey, they have Elizabeth."

"Excuse me?"

"Elizabeth's in Paris. Somebody kidnapped her."

Audrey clutched Peck's upper arms and pushed him away so as to look in his face.

"Who would do that?"

"I don't know."

"Have they hurt her?"

"She's in Paris and kidnapped. That's all I know."

"No!" Audrey screamed.

"I need a reading, bad. I need to clear my head, think straight. I need help knowing what to do."

"Have they harmed her?"

"I don't think so, but they're threatening if I don't do what they tell me to do."

Audrey locked the door.

"Kitchen," Audrey said.

They stepped through two rooms and into the kitchen. A tarot deck was sitting on the porcelain table top.

"My kitchen is Elizabeth's favorite room," Audrey said. "Her spirit will guide us."

She gestured Peck to sit. She pulled a chair and sat.

Audrey took Peck's hands into hers.

"Boudreaux, tell me everything."

"I've been here in Baton Rouge. All week I've been packing Elizabeth's things for her move to Paris. The day before yesterday I drove her to the airport. She was going to stay in a hotel in Paris while she looked for an apartment—and then she was going to call and tell me where to ship things."

Peck recounted his time in the confessional with Father McBride and the aftermath of being followed from the basilica and threatened. He buried his face in his hands.

"I should have gone to Paris with her. She'd be safe if I had gone with her."

"Boudreaux, shuffle the cards. I selected a French deck. I had a feeling come over me when you called. This is the deck we should use. I want you to take it with you when you leave—until Elizabeth is safe."

"The man who threatened me is French."

"Boudreaux, take the deck out of its packing."

Peck obliged.

"Call me Peck, Audrey? Elizabeth likes Peck."

Audrey nodded.

"Set the deck on the table."

He obliged.

"Bring your energy, Peck. Knock on it."

Peck counted three knuckle taps on the deck.

"Was that three?" Audrey asked.

"Ah *oui*."

"Divide the deck into three piles."

Peck cut the deck and placed it in three stacks.

"Now put the piles together and shuffle them."

Peck shuffled. He set the cards on the table.

"I'm lifting the top card," Audrey said. "That card will be a summary of our reading. It will point the way. She lifted the card and placed it face down in front of her.

"Please fan the deck out, Peck."

Peck obliged, spreading the deck across the table top.

"Select two cards."

Peck floated his palm back and forth over the fan of tarot cards, pointed at one and pushed it out. He repeated his hand float, pointed at a second and pushed it out.

"These two, Audrey. The first one for Elizabeth and this other for me."

"We're ready, then," Audrey said.

She turned the card she had taken from the top.

"Oh my," Audrey said.

"What's wrong?" Peck asked.

"It's *The Fool* card, Peck."

"What's it mean?" Peck asked.

"You are dealing with a complete fool, Peck. This could be very dangerous. *The Fool* is a beggar. He's a vagabond—wears ragged clothes, goes shoeless, carries a stick in his hand."

"Audrey, the voodoo man had a big rosary over his arm and a long snake in his hand."

"The man who threatened you?"

"Ah *oui*."

"Not here in Baton Rouge, but in New Orleans?"

"Ah *oui*."

"Last night?"

"Ah *oui*."

"'The Fool' means new beginnings. It means not knowing what to expect; it means improvising and believing in the universe. Does this sound like the Frenchman."

"Nah, nah. The voodoo man knew what he wanted."

"*The Fool* could be someone in Paris, then, holding Elizabeth."

"You really think, Audrey?"

"It could mean that regardless how professional and efficient they appear to be, their motives could be flawed. They could be actors with no knowledge of what they are scheming to do, which could hinder their ability to execute."

"Are you saying it's like maybe they've never done something like this before and could make mistakes?"

"I feel certain of it, Peck. Big mistakes."

"So do I," Peck said.

"Peck, if this voodoo man is a puppet for someone, clumsiness could cost him his life."

"He tripped on bootlaces—fell in the parking lot."

"Interesting."

"Ah *oui*."

"The reverse of *The Fool* is *Chaos*, Peck. We always look at the reverse of cards. The reverse here is lack of direction, poor judgement, stupidity."

"They'd hurt Elizabeth—if he orders it," Peck said.

"Turn one of your two cards, Peck."

Peck turned *The Tower* card.

"A dangerous card. *The Tower* means something or someone will be left behind, Peck."

"For real?" Peck asked.

"*The Tower* means that painful endings may be a necessary step to take. You may have to sacrifice."

"I'll be ready."

"Be careful what you tell the man, Peck. A warned man counts for two."

"I'll be careful what I say."

Audrey turned Peck's other card.

"*Knight of Swords*—oh my," Audrey said.

She cupped her mouth, trying to gather her thoughts.

"What's wrong, Audrey? Is it a bad one?"

"*Knight of Swords* speaks of something sudden. It could be poorly planned, like *The Fool* card indicates, but *Knight of Swords* warns it could be violent, dangerous … and anger that cannot be reasoned with."

"I have to stay strong, Audrey."

"Peck, this is a time for you to stay calm. You find strength through serenity. Keep your mind active by thinking alternatives—but positive alternatives. One positive trait of the *Knight of Swords* is it can announce a fight you can and will win."

Peck made a sign of the cross and kissed his thumb.

"This was telling, Peck. You'll benefit from this reading."

"Thank you, Audrey."

"These people are up to no good, Peck, but I read a sense that they're making things up as they go. They're tempting, threatening, and for what—to get you to do their bidding. It's obvious, but they're making a big theatrical event out of it for some reason. The man could as easily have said there's something we want you to do, then tell you what they want you to do, and then said 'do it and we'll turn Elizabeth loose.'"

"Ah *oui*—for sure."

"It's in the cards, Peck. It's all in the cards."

"*Aye yi-yi*," Peck whispered.

"It's up to you now, Peck. Elizabeth's counting on you. A master dealing with scoundrels. Be careful."

"I will."

"And call me the second Elizabeth is safe."

"I will, I promise."

Chapter 7

Peck climbed into his pickup and pulled the door shut. A text signaled on his iPhone.

It was a text from the voodoo man.

"It's him," Peck said.

"Who?" Aurelie asked.

"The voodoo man. The kidnapper."

"Can I see?" Aurelie asked.

Peck nodded.

Aurelie leaned over to read the text with Peck.

"Le colis est-il toujours avec vous ? Sûr?" voodoo man texted. ("Is the package still with you? Safe?")

Peck knew his strength would show by brief answers, but he was smart enough to know to tell the truth—not chance getting caught in a lie.

"Je l'ai dans un endroit sûr," Peck texted. *("I have it in a safe place.")*

"Avez vous un passeport?" voodoo man texted. ("Do you have a passport?")

"Mais non, non passeport." (No passport.")

"Prends en un. Envoyez-moi un SMS avant midi demain, exactement quand vous l'aurez en main—et ne retardez pas ou ne traînez pas les pieds pour en obtenir un. Comprenez vous?" voodoo man texted. ("Get one. Text me by noon tomorrow exactly when you will have it in hand—and do not stall or drag your feet in getting one. Do you understand?")

Peck pointed at the text about his needing a passport, He looked at Aurelie.

"They've got Elizabeth. Why else would I need a passport if they didn't have her?" Peck asked.

"I think you're right, Peck," Aurelie said.

Peck tapped a text to voodoo man:

"Je veux savoir qu'elle est vivante," ("I want to know she's alive.")

"Attendez." voodoo man texted. ("Wait.")

Minutes went by. Peck's phone rang, but it was the voodoo man calling, not texting.

"What?" Peck asked.

"Monsieur, in thirty seconds you will receive a call. You will not answer it. You will let her leave a message. If you answer the phone and try to speak to her, you will never see her again. Do you understand?"

"I understand."

"Text me immediately after the call and you're satisfied." Voodoo man clicked off.

Within seconds an incoming call appeared on his screen, calling his iPhone. He didn't know the number but he let it ring through to *voice mail* and waited for the signal. The tone sounded that he had a voice mail message. He turned on the speaker and listened:

A female voice barked.

"Dites-lui simplement que vous allez bien et raccrochez !" ("Just tell him you're okay and hang up!")

Peck could hear an echo with the voice.

"Boudreaux," Elizabeth said. "This is Elizabeth. I don't know what's happening. It's very dark."

He could hear Elizabeth asking someone a question. It was Elizabeth's voice. She asked in French.

"Puis-je s'il vous plaît lui demander de dire à ma sœur que je vais bien?" ("Can I please ask him to tell my sister that I'm okay?")

"Oui. Vite! Mais pas un mot de plus!" the female voice barked. ("Yes. Quickly! But not another word!")

"Merci. Peck, s'il te plaît, dis à ma sœur, Gudule, de ne pas s'inquiéter. Trois cent quarante-huit, six un neuf. Je dois partir. Je t'aime," Elizabeth said. ("Thank you. Peck, please tell my sister, Gudule, not to worry. Three hundred forty-eight, six-one-nine. I have to go now. I love you.")

The message ended. Peck texted voodoo man:

"I'll text you by noon tomorrow about my passport."

The voodoo man didn't respond.

Peck grabbed the steering wheel with a grip of helpless frustration. Aurelie watched, not interrupting his thoughts. Peck began mumbling to himself.

"She's okay," he mumbled.

"What was the echo?" Aurelie asked.

"Clues, I must listen for clues. Elizabeth is smart."

Peck picked up his phone and touched Lily Cup's number.

"Peck? Where are you? Larry told me—"

"I need a passport."

"Are you okay?"

"I need it fast, cher."

"I have your birth certificate."

"What do I have to do to get one?"

"I know your signature. I could fill out the application and sign it."

"That would be good, thanks, cher."

"I'll do an expedited application," Lily Cup said. "You'll need your passport picture taken. I'll text you places you can go. Where are you?"

"I have to call Larry," Peck said.

He clicked off, distracted, and ended the call with Lily Cup. He touched Larry's code number on his phone.

"Talk to me," Larry said.

"The voodoo man told me to get a passport."

"Did you make him prove Elizabeth was okay?"

"Ah *oui*. She called on somebody's phone and left a message on my phone. I wasn't allowed to talk, just listen. I have her message."

"You will be his mule, by the sound of it," Larry said.

"Lily Cup is getting my passport. I have to tell him by noon tomorrow when I'll have it."

"Any read? Any clues in her phone message, Peck?"

"Yes—have to study it. I think more than one."

"You need some time to do your tracking thing, Peck. I'll get Lily Cup to stall the passport a couple of days."

"That sounds good, Larry. Get her to text me when I'll be able to have it in my hand. You decide when, but tell me so I can send him a text by noon tomorrow."

"I will," Larry said. "Go do your thing, Peck."

"You okay, frien', with the wife and kids?" Peck asked.

"My boys are my life. I'm good about where I am now. I'm keeping my head clear."

"You're a good man, Larry."

"Peck, I'm wanting the coroner, Chris O'Sullivan, to x-ray the black box—see if there're any hidden secrets wrapped in that canvas."

"Good idea, Larry."

"Problem is getting it out of Charlie's Blue Note and to the morgue without being seen. They may have followed you the night you brought it there."

"Ah *oui*."

"We'll figure something out. Are you with Mammas?"

"Going there now. I had my tarot reading. Got my frien' Aurelie and her computer. We're going to do some tracking, eat some crab, and suck some tail."

"Stay safe, Peck—be in touch. I'll keep you posted."

"Get Lily Cup to text me when I can get a passport, Larry. I have to tell him when I'll have one by noon tomorrow."

"You're starting to repeat yourself, my friend," Larry said. "Better get some rest."

"At Mammas. I will, Larry."

"And don't forget to make him prove she's alive every time you talk or text or whatever it is you do."

"I won't forget."

The call ended. Peck stared at nothing through the windshield.

"Aurelie?" he asked.

"What?" Aurelie asked.

"What time is it in Paris?"

"You mean now?"

"Ah *oui*."

Aurelie looked at her iPhone. "It's 5:48 in the afternoon in Paris right this minute."

"That means it's daylight there?"

Aurelie studied a webpage on her iPhone.

"Sunset isn't for two more hours. It's daylight in Paris."

"Thanks, bébé."

"What's the difference, day or night in Paris, Peck?"

"Elizabeth said she was in the dark," Peck said.

"That's right, she did."

"She said it was very dark."

Peck touched Baitman Alex's number on his iPhone.

"Where are you, my friend?" Baitman Alex asked.

"Leaving Baton Rouge and heading to Mammas, frien'."

"Ha! Your mammas was right."

"How's that?"

"She told me you'd be coming today. I went early and tossed the traps—five on either side of the houseboat. We'll have us a boil when you get there, for sure."

"Are you there now?" Peck asked.

"I'm in my bait trailer, reading a book, selling some bait. Fish guts are going good today—must be a run on the catfish, Peck. Want me to bring my rods?"

"Not this time, Baitman Alex. Bring your lady. We'll have us some fun, but I got tracking to do. See you at Mammas."

Peck ended the call and drove off.

"Are you okay, Peck?" Aurelie asked.

"Elizabeth said some numbers, bébé. Was it a phone number? I don't like not knowing."

"I bet it's a clue, Peck. You'll figure it out. I'll help."

"You're right. Everything's going to be good. We'll find some more clues."

"Can we sleep together?"

"For true, if you want. We're friens', bébé. We've slept together before."

"Will Mammas be okay with it?"

He answered by squeezing her thigh. He was distracted with thoughts of Audrey's reading, the message from Elizabeth in Paris, and the short white marker lines on the highway passing below.

"Elizabeth doesn't have a sister," Peck said.

Chapter 8

As Peck and Aurelie left Baton Rouge for Mammas in New Orleans, Charlie was pulling the Blue Note door open.

"Come in, Larry. They're all here," Charlie said.

Charlie locked the door behind them. The Blue Note wouldn't open to the public until five.

"Peck's at Mammas's or on his way," Larry said.

"The rest of the gang's here, Larry. Some of your team too—Coroner O'Sullivan, Locksmith Lizzie, and Officer Downs."

"Thank you, Charlie. Thanks for making this happen."

"How's Peck holding up?" Charlie asked.

"He's doing fine. You know, his early life was filled with dark mysteries and abuse, so this'll be another walk in the park for our friend," Larry said.

"I don't envy who's behind this—kidnapping Elizabeth," Charlie said.

"You've got that right. Nobody fucks with Peck's friends or their families and gets away with it. The voodoo man is one weasel who just made a wrong turn into a dead-end alley."

Larry and Charlie went to where everyone sat around four tables put together. On the table lay a tray of warm cinnamon buns and thermoses filled with chicory. Larry greeted each in turn, shaking hands—Gabe, Sasha, Lily Cup, Officer Downs, Locksmith Lizzie and the coroner, Chris O'Sullivan.

Then Larry held up a finger to excuse himself.

"Give me a minute, folks," he said.

He walked back to the dark kitchen, likely to get the wooden box. As he returned, Charlie made an announcement.

"Everybody?"

Everyone looked up.

"I called Mayor Cantrell this morning, folks," Charlie said. "I told her what's going down, and how it all began at the Cathedral Basilica on Bastille Day."

"What'd the mayor have to say?" Lily Cup asked.

"In strictest confidence, she told me to keep her informed, and if we needed help here or in France to let her know."

"She's a good egg," Gabe said.

Larry set the wooden box on the table.

"Ladies and gents, the mystery box," Larry said.

"Slow down, my brother. Have you talked to Peck?" Gabe asked. "Last night he wasn't sure. Does he know now if someone was kidnapped—and if so, who?"

"Confirmed this morning, Gabe. They've got Elizabeth, and she's in Paris," Larry said.

"Is she okay?" Sasha asked.

"Peck confirmed this morning that Elizabeth is unharmed—but she has been kidnapped," Larry said. "That has been confirmed."

"He was in his teens when he and Elizabeth met," Lily Cup said. "Peck used to walk twelve miles barefoot from Carencro where he mowed the lawns, way over to where he met Elizabeth in Anse La Butte. They took a fancy to each other, and he'd walk that eleven miles weekly to spend a few hours with her. She was working in a kitchen at a Cajun chicken place in Breaux Bridge. I know Elizabeth. She speaks fluent French, and I know for a fact she won't be afraid to make things happen for herself. I can't see her being intimidated. I think she'll figure the spot she's in—Peck's limitations and a way to signal Peck—"

"And he'll figure a way to communicate with her," Gabe said.

"It's goodbye voodoo man—bet on it," Lily Cup said.

Larry told the story of how the box got in Peck's truck, of Peck bringing it to Charlie's, and how they opened it, and what they found and didn't find.

"Have you checked it for bugs, Larry?" Lily Cup asked.

"It has no recording devices in it," Locksmith Lizzie said.

"Any tracking device, Larry?" Chris, asked.

"That we don't know, Chris," Larry said.

"That's why we asked you all to come," Charlie said. "We didn't want to move it unnecessarily until we know for certain it doesn't have a tracking bug."

"That's smart," Gabe said. "If they're tracking it, and you give them a trail of different addresses moving it around, you'd make it easy for them to build a wall of defense."

"That'd give the bastards confidence," Lily Cup said.

"Let me show you its inside," Larry said. "Lizzie, will you do the honors?"

Lizzie took a sheet of paper from her purse and unfolded it. Reading combinations she'd written down the night before, she opened every padlock and set them on the table in order.

"There you go, Lieutenant."

Larry opened the case and rested the top back on its hinges.

"Don't touch anything, folks, but have a close look. It might be booby-trapped," Larry said.

"This is not an everyday, store-bought box," Charlie said.

"Whoever designed this was a craftsman. It's beautiful," Sasha said. "I have jewelry boxes that aren't this nice."

"That could be a clue, Larry. You might jot it down," Gabe said.

"How's that a clue?" Larry asked.

"Gabe's right, Larry. Look at how well it's built," Sasha said. "It's even got corduroy velvet lining with expensive silk thread and hand stitching."

"I bet there's a dozen coats of rubbed lacquer," Gabe said.

Sasha pointed at an interior wall of the box.

"Look. The base is some kind of some rare hardwood, and this lid—it looks like cedar. This thing is a masterpiece."

"Are you guys saying that whoever's behind this whole nightmare charade is an artist because of how this box is built?" Larry asked.

"Look at its detail, Larry," Lily Cup said. "Only an OCD artist type would be crazy enough to build a fucking box like this just for a heist or for smuggling or whatever he's up to—excuse my French, Lizzie."

"No apologies necessary," Lizzie said. "And it's definitely a nightmare, Lieutenant Gaines. It's not a charade. I watched Peck's eyes last night in the kitchen when you lifted it out of the closet."

"Inside it," Sasha said, "those are beautiful gold frames—hand carved and etched or engraved."

"Fourteen of them," Gabe said.

"Fourteen?" Lily Cup asked.

"Peck suggested we not try to pull any out, as they might be booby-trapped," Larry said.

"Fourteen gold frames—if they are frames," Gabe said.

"Are they plated or solid gold?" Sasha asked.

"By the weight of the box, they have to be plated. It'd be a lot heavier if they were solid gold," Larry said.

"Whatever they are, that's 24 carats," Gabe said.

"Listen to you. You're good, dancing man," Sasha said.

"Brothers know gold, darlin'," Gabe mused.

"Stations of the Cross," Lily Cup said.

"Explain," Larry replied.

"On walls of a church there are fourteen Stations of the Cross."

"Every church, hon?"

"I don't know about every church, Larry—but every Catholic church. All the same—well, they're not the same picture, but fourteen of the same stations with pictures painted by different artists with captions about something that happened on the day of the crucifixion. Like *Jesus falls the first time*."

"It's maybe a Basilica thing?" Larry asked.

"Usually they have crosses on top. If these are Stations of the Cross, they might be in this box, upside down," Lily Cup said.

"These could be valuable and stolen—" Chris started.

"And the voodoo man needs a mule to smuggle them out of the country," Larry finished.

"Peck for his mule," Chris said. "If these are legitimate."

"If they're stolen from the Cathedral Basilica, we can't risk tipping the voodoo man that we've opened the box by asking a priest if the Basilica is missing some gold Stations of the Cross," Larry said.

"Little sister," Gabe said, "how do you know it's fourteen in every church and they aren't changed up from time to time, like with Holidays—"

"And Holy Days of Obligation, like that?" Sasha asked. "Gabe's right, Lily Cup. They could be souvenirs from a local flea market."

"Smuggle flea market souvenirs into Paris? Give me a break," Lily Cup said.

"Well …" Sasha started.

"I can't believe you guys—what you don't know," Lily Cup said. The Catholic Mass is about one thing—the 'this is my body and this is my blood' thing—remembering Christ's sacrifice. The Stations of the Cross aren't fucking political cartoons or holiday comics. They are the day Jesus was condemned to death and crucified on the cross."

"Jesus," Sasha said. "Don't get your panties in a knot."

"I know it's fourteen, Sasha. First off, because the Catholic church never changes anything. It's the Protestants who changed the Catholic church. That's why they're called Protestants. Second, you were never good at math, Sasha, so zip it."

"Don't be fresh, Missy. I got B's in math and English."

"I don't know how. Your brain stops counting at 36 D—"

"*Hee hee,*" Gabe snickered.

"I need a martini?" Sasha asked.

Charlie stood to go to the bar.

Lily Cup blurted out, "I know it's fourteen because the first time I went down on a boy I was in a closet in study hall and my penance was I had to visit every Station of the Cross and say one *Our Father* and one *Hail Mary* to all fourteen—before school for fourteen days—and Father was there every morning watching."

"You confessed a BJ, little sister?" Gabe asked.

"It was my first. I liked it. Figured if I liked it, it had to be a mortal sin."

"I thought I heard all the stories," Sasha said.

"It was Ronnie Applegate, your Junior Prom date, Sasha."

"Why you little—" Sasha started.

"I never told you."

Sasha guffawed and slapped the table with her hand. Charlie handed her a martini and sat down.

"Fourteen has always been my unlucky number," Lily Cup said.

"It's think time, folks," Larry said. "Any ideas?"

"I think these French guys have been following Peck in Baton Rouge," Gabe said.

"Give me some facts to back it," Larry replied.

"One—Elizabeth lived in Baton Rouge. She has never been to New Orleans—at least with Peck she hasn't. Two—if she was grabbed in Paris, how would the kidnapper know she was flying to Paris and what flight she'd be on if he wasn't tracking her cell phone."

"How do we know she went to Paris? She could still be here," Chris O'Sullivan said.

"She left a message on Peck's phone," Larry said.

"She did?" Gabe asked.

"If it was from her iPhone, that proves she's been kidnapped, but it doesn't prove she's in Paris," Sasha said.

"It wasn't from her iPhone," Larry said.

"She went to Paris," Lily Cup said. "Peck watched her get on the plane and he watched the plane back out of the gate."

"Without all the cloak and dagger, it could be the kidnapper overheard her in conversation about moving to Paris maybe at the restaurant where she worked in Baton

Rouge, or maybe listened to her making a phone call from there," Larry said. "Our imaginations could be thinking it started in Paris."

"Could be that, Larry. But how would he know he could find Peck at Cathedral-Basilica?" Gabe asked.

"And on Bastille Day?" Chris asked.

"Maybe he knew Peck's habits?"

"Peck has no habits," Lily Cup said.

"He does have a routine, little sister. Maybe this voodoo man knew his routine? Of Confession, Mass, Communion."

"Okay then, but shooting holes in that—his routine is First Friday of the month, Gabe," Larry said. "First Friday was last week, not yesterday."

"Touché, my brother," Gabe said.

"How did he know Peck would be in church yesterday?" Larry asked.

"Are we assuming Peck has never seen his face? He was wearing a mask, correct, Lieutenant?" Chris asked.

"That's correct," Larry said.

"So, if the same man was unmasked and in plain clothes, he could have easily followed Peck," Chris said.

"But if he followed him that night, Chris, he'd be in his voodoo costume," Larry said.

"Not necessarily, Lieutenant."

"What's your point, Chris?"

"He could have followed Peck while in plain clothes and changed into his costume in a men's room while Peck was attending Mass or in the Confessional," Chris said.

"Peck would certainly know if someone was following him from Baton Rouge to New Orleans and the Basilica," Gabe said. "He'd sense it within a mile and pull over."

"He'd know it for sure," Larry said. "Gabe's right."

"So, if he wasn't followed, how'd he learn where Peck was going to be and when?" Sasha asked.

"I'm thinking the voodoo man might be a stalker of the Cathedral-Basilica," Larry said. "We're planting him in Baton

Rouge. Let's maybe plant him in New Orleans and work backwards."

"That's turning a pocket inside out—I like it," Gabe said.

"Lieutenant, I suggest we take pictures of the box, and we check with smaller, home-based woodworkers or cabinet makers," Chris said.

"Where?" Larry asked.

"I'd start in Baton Rouge—then New Orleans if the Baton Rouge search comes up empty handed," Chris said.

"I'm not allowed to leave this jurisdiction," Larry said.

"I can," Lily Cup said.

"Lily Cup, if you do it, be careful to only call on the small, cottage workshop carpenters or cabinet makers. Not the big guys," Chris said.

"Why not the big guys? Why not all of them?" Lily Cup asked.

"Yes, why not, Chris?" Larry asked. "Can't be that many."

"There are reasons why she shouldn't call on the big guys, Lieutenant. As magnificent as this box is, it was constructed quickly. It still has a lacquer smell. If a legitimate, large wood working or cabinet shop was asked to bid on it or to make it, it would have taken months, with red tape and material back orders they'd have to go through, requiring voodoo man's approval along every step of the way."

"What's your point, Chris?" Larry asked.

"I see his point, Larry," Gabe said.

"Want to share?" Larry asked.

"Big shops have more sophisticated communications than simple handyman carpenters," Gabe said. "If somebody in a big shop took it on as a money *under the table* job that his boss didn't know about ..." Gabe started.

"And someone snooped around asking about the box, that snoop may get voodoo man called, and tipped—and Elizabeth dead."

"I see your point," Larry said.

"Add to that, Lieutenant, we know something's hidden in the top of this box—under the handle," Lizzie said.

"We're pretty certain there is," Larry said.

"Unless there was a money under the table scenario like Gabe thinks, the large cabinet makers or shops would never risk losing city or state government projects by knowingly building something that's obviously going to be used for smuggling," Chris said.

"Lily Cup," Larry said, "they're right. I think cottage workshop carpenters only."

"How do I approach them without their suspecting me of being a cop?"

"Little sister is right, Larry," Gabe said. "How can she walk in and not signal she's investigating?"

"Just walk in, show them the picture. Don't ask if they built it—just say you want one like it and ask if they can do it," Larry said.

"Perfect," Chris said.

"You might have a few big bills in your paw when you ask," Gabe said.

"Hundreds might scare them, cause them to pause and look. Grants they know—Benjamins maybe not," Chris said.

"I'll have fifties in my hand," Lily Cup said.

"We need to find somebody in Paris who can do some undercover work for us there. This could get dangerous and we need to be represented there," Larry said.

"How about Peck going?" Gabe asked. "He speaks the language."

"You're right, and Peck would get on top of things quickly if he were there," Larry said.

Lily Cup rapped on the table with her knuckles, catching Sasha's eye.

"What?" Sasha asked.

"You've been on your cell this whole time. Have you heard a word we were saying?" Lily Cup asked.

"I was making reservations—sorry. Where were we?"

"We were talking about how—wait a minute—what reservations? For what?"

"I leave in the morning."

"For where?" Lily Cup asked.

"The last thing any of us should say out loud from here on out would be our people's names. We have no idea who among us is being bugged, what's being recorded and who's chasing whom," Sasha said.

"Reservations for where?"

"I'll be at the Z."

"The where?"

Sasha mouthed "*Paris*."

"Paris?!"

"You two don't have to whisper. There are no bugs in here," Lizzie said.

"Larry, I'll be waiting for your instructions in Paris," Sasha said. "I've had defense training. I know how to open doors and I know how to get people to talk. Let me go to Paris."

"That's not a bad idea—maybe a good strategy. Boots on the ground in enemy territory," Gabe said.

"Gabe's right," Chris added.

"Imagine, Sasha being there long enough to assimilate. She'll blend into the crowd unnoticed before anything happens," Gabe said.

"Lily Cup?" Larry asked.

"What?"

"You should go, too," Larry said.

"Huh?"

"You both speak French."

"I hate speaking French."

"You both could do some snooping around Paris with no one getting wise."

"Two chicks, snooping around Paris—would they stick out, ya' think, Larry?" Gabe asked.

"Ladies, you could go as a couple—hold hands," Larry jested.

"What!?" Lily Cup demanded with a guffaw. "Me give up"—(she pointed at Larry's crotch)—"cigars?"

Everyone howled.

"Who'll check cabinet makers, Larry?" Lily Cup asked.

"You can buy Cuban cigars in Paris," Larry said.

"Why don't I go to Paris after I do Baton Rouge?" Lily Cup asked.

"Lieutenant, in three days may I take a day of my vacation?" Officer Downs asked.

"Now?" Larry asked. "In the middle of—"

"I need to go to Baton Rouge, Lieutenant, and do some snooping around small carpenters and cabinet makers. I'll do it on my own time," Officer Downs said.

Larry smiled.

"Why in three days, Downs?"

"I'll need two days to let my whiskers grow to a stubble, Lieutenant … I don't want to walk in looking like a cop."

"See why I love this guy, folks?" Larry asked. "This man here, Officer Downs, is the best cop I know—not only because he's a good cop, but because he always wants to be the best there is. If my friend and loyal compadre here sees something that needs doing, he gets it done. You can take it to the bank."

"We've got to save Elizabeth," Officer Downs said.

"I made your reservations, Lily Cup," Sasha said.

"Larry, tell Peck he can pick up his passport here at Charlie's … in three days," Lily Cup said.

"Three days is good. It'll give us time to maneuver. I'll tell him. Are you certain you'll have it by then?"

"I'll have it this afternoon, Larry. I know a guy."

Chris was stuffing a cinnamon bun in his mouth when his iPhone vibrated. He lifted it from his pocket and read the text message.

"Uh-oh," he muttered.

Larry's two-way squawked.

"Unit nine-eight-four, this is headquarters."

"Copy, headquarters. This is unit nine-eight-four," Larry said.

"Unit nine-eight-four, what's your position?"

"This is unit nine-eight-four, headquarters. I'm at one-two-three Frenchman Street."

"Unit nine-eight-four, we have a floater in the canal at Holy Cross—Sister and Burgundy. You copy?"

"A body in the canal—Sister Street and Burgundy Street—copy that. On my way, headquarters. Over."

"I'll follow you, Lieutenant," Chris said.

Larry pushed his two-way button.

"Headquarters this is unit nine-eight-four."

"Unit nine-eight-four, this is headquarters. We read you."

"Coroner O'Sullivan will follow me to the scene. Do you copy?"

"Copy that," headquarters squawked. *"Three officers are at the scene, taping. Over and out."*

"Lieutenant, ask them if the floater is face down, Chris said.

"Headquarters, Coroner O'Sullivan asks—is the floater face down? Do you copy?"

"That's affirmative, nine-eight-four. The floater is face down."

"Tell them not to move it," Chris said.

"Headquarters, Coroner O'Sullivan asks not to move the body until we get there Do you copy?"

"That's affirmative nine-eight-four."

Larry turned to the table of friends.

"Folks, Chris and I have some work to do," Larry said. "Can we meet here later today to talk more about the Peck–Elizabeth scenario?"

"What's on your mind, Larry?" Gabe asked.

"What's on my mind, Gabe, is kind of like the Battle of New Orleans. The enemy has us boxed in in too many corners, behind too many bushes. We've got three playing fields to contend with—one here in New Orleans, a second one in Baton Rouge, and a third in Paris. I don't like three playing fields. I like home court advantage."

"Got a tactic, Larry?" Gabe asked.

"To figure a way to level the playing fields."

"Three o'clock, here at Charlie's," Gabe said.

Everyone agreed.

Chapter 9

As the meeting at Charlie's Blue Note broke up, Peck was parking under the weeping willow he'd seen grow since he watched Mammas planting it when he was a baby from a highchair on the houseboat. The houseboat had been tied to it for near a quarter century by a nylon rope the tree had since grown over and embedded it at its heart.

Baitman Alex sat on the ground past the ten anchored ropes that were attached to crab traps he'd tossed hours before. He was reading a book, paying no mind to the pickup approaching or of Peck getting out. His wife was on the houseboat with Mammas, having tea.

"Baitman Alex, how you are, my frien'?"

Baitman Alex looked up, squinted in the sun, marked his page, and stood up. They hugged liked brothers, always happy to see each other.

"Baitman Alex, meet my frien', Aurelie."

"Welcome to you," Baitman Alex said.

"I'm here to help Peck do research," Aurelie said. "Nice to meet you, too, Baitman Alex."

"Are you tracking something, Peck?' Baitman Alex asked.

"Something big, frien'. I'll tell you when we eat."

"We'll have a good boil, Peck. I pulled on a trap, already three crabs in it—tossed it back in," Baitman Alex said.

"You'll like Mammas, bébé," Peck said. "Let's go have you meet everybody and then we'll get busy tracking clues."

"Peck, why don't we go in, and I'll meet everyone, but then you lie down and try to get some rest, like Larry said? Then we can work."

"You heard Larry tell me that?"

"I did—he was pretty loud, Peck. He said you'll be no good at your tracking thing if you can't keep your eyes open."

"Baitman Alex, I've got to get some rest then we'll get together. You mind, frien'?"

"I've got reading to do—no worries—sleep."

"I'm thinking thirty, forty minutes maybe. Read your book, frien'. I'll take Aurelie in and say hello to Mammas and your lady."

As they turned to get to the ladder on the houseboat, Baitman Alex squatted and opened his book.

"I still have two-hundred-thirty pages to go. See you when you get up."

Peck waved at him. "Let's go in, bébé."

They climbed on the deck and stepped into the houseboat. Aurelie was introduced to Baitman Alex's lady and given the tour and told by Mammas that the feather bed in the back bedroom was hers and Peck's bunk. She would sleep on a comfortable pull-out in the main saloon.

"How do you know my Boudreaux?" Mammas asked.

"We're just friends, Mammas. I work at a phone store on Canal Street. One day Peck came in looking for phones. He and I started talking, and we found out he'd grown up in Carencro and I grew up nearby over in Church Point—and we're both Cajun French. Seems we hit it off right away, Mammas. Sometimes we go dance the Zydeco, sometimes I'll cook him a creole something. We're friends, pretty much."

"Honey, is everything okay with my Boudreaux?" Mammas asked.

"Why do you ask, Mammas?"

"He had worried eyes, my boy. That's not like him."

"Mammas, why don't we wait until he wakes up. I'm sure he'll want to tell whatever's going on in that head of his."

"You're right. We'll let the boy rest."

"Can I help, Mammas? I'm good in the kitchen. How can I help?"

"That's sweet of you offering, Aurelie."

"Please, give me a task. I would love to help."

"I know Baitman Alex will need firewood, Aurelie. You might let me catch up with my friend here over our tea and you could go see if he needs help stacking twigs and branches for the boil."

Aurelie smiled, stepped from the saloon and climbed off the houseboat. Without interrupting Baitman Alex, she began gathering and stacking twigs and fallen branches.

Chapter 10

Larry pulled to the curb on Sister Street, switched his emergency signals on to flash as Chris pulled in behind him. A small crowd had gathered on the street and grass near the edge of the canal. Larry clipped his badge to his suit pocket and climbed out of his car.

"Folks, I'll have to ask you to step back," Larry said. "Officers, secure the area."

An officer walked to the crowd with his arms spread.

"Folks, this area is being taped as a possible crime scene. We don't want to contaminate evidence. Please step back—over there near Burgundy Street would be good."

Larry held his arms out in concurrence, gesturing to the gatherers to move away.

"Any witnesses?" Larry asked the crowd. "Folks, if you saw anything suspicious or witnessed some goings on that might have caused this lady to die, we'd appreciate a statement. We will keep the source confidential. That's a promise. Please give it some thought."

Chris and Larry stepped to the canal where two uniformed police officers stood guard.

"Officers, what do we have?" Larry asked.

"A floater, Lieutenant. Looks like a female. That's all we know now. I called it in and we've been waiting orders," Officer Milton said. "She was face down, so we didn't touch anything."

"Officer Milton, give a hand and help keep Coroner O'Sullivan here from falling into the canal while he takes a closer look."

"Yes, Lieutenant."

Officer Milton offered his hand to Chris.

"I'll hang on to you, Coroner."

"Who discovered the body?" Larry asked.

"Lieutenant, Cadet Bergeron was the first one on the scene. He spotted the body from his bicycle. He'd be the best one to tell you what he saw."

"Chris, let me know if there's any identification."

"Will do, Lieutenant."

"Cadet Bergeron, you were on a bike?" Larry asked.

"I was riding home from work, Lieutenant. I live a couple blocks from here."

"No car?"

"Not on festival days, Lieutenant. it's easier to ride my bike to and from work."

"This neighborhood's some pretty nice digs on cop pay, Cadet—good on you, son," Larry said.

"I live with my aunt, Lieutenant. It's her house. I rent a room, is all. I'm looking to move—saving up for it."

"Is your aunt a good cook, son?"

"The best, Lieutenant— used to work at Brennan's."

Larry moved toward the shore. "What's the scoop, Cadet. Walk me through it."

"Lieutenant, like I said, I was riding home from work and was over there on St. Claude, sir, on the bridge. There was hardly any traffic so I was doing some looking around—you know how you do when you're on a bike, looking in store windows and at people?"

"I know," Larry said. "Is there usually a lot of traffic on that route home?"

"Most times, Lieutenant, but being Bastille Day, everyone was in the Quarter or on Canal Street, is my guess, walking, not driving, sir."

"Go on, Cadet."

"I was crossing the bridge, looked over here and thought I saw something. It was like a dark bump in the canal with ripples around it and the canal was usually smooth and calm, Lieutenant, unless it's raining. I could tell it was a body floating at the shore line."

"Good eyes, Cadet."

"I rode right to here, Lieutenant I jumped off my bike and ran to the edge."

"And you found what you first thought—"

"It was a body, Lieutenant."

"Coroner O'Sullivan?" Larry asked.

"Lieutenant, we have a Caucasian female, dead, my guess, twenty hours. I need to get her on land," Chris said.

They rested the body on the grass. Chris knelt and searched the body.

"No identification. Unless we find something, she'll be tagged Jane Doe, Lieutenant. We'll run prints. If that tells us nothing we'll see if someone reports her missing."

"Bastille Day partier, Coroner Sullivan?"

"This lady isn't in costume, Lieutenant."

"Any visible cause of death, Chris?"

"Too early to tell, Lieutenant. No visible bullet or puncture wounds. This isn't a place to make assumptions. I need to get her on ice."

"Any timetable?" Larry asked.

"I've got an autopsy working—an exhumation for a court trial. I should be able to get to her tomorrow...."

"Thank you, Chris."

"But one thing is certain, Lieutenant."

"Which is?"

"Our Jane Doe here has something tied around her waist that's not a part of her dress."

Larry pointed his flashlight at the body.

"What the hell is that, Chris? I can't tell."

"Too many prying eyes, Lieutenant. Let's give her some respect and get her to the morgue. Forensics gets the first look."

"Roger that, Chris—call me," Larry said.

"Maybe it was tied to an anchor that came loose."

"That'd make it a murder," Larry said.

"Lieutenant, you might consider dragging the canal to see what might be down there."

"Good thinking, Chris."

"Can you move the crowd, Lieutenant? We'll have the scene photographed, and I'll start the autopsy tomorrow."

"Good man, Chris."

"I might have to miss our meeting at Charlie's this afternoon, Lieutenant. Keep me posted, please?"

"I will. You keep me posted on anything you find out about our floater here."

"I will, Lieutenant."

"Officers," Larry said. "After the body is bagged and out of here, I want this entire shoreline combed for possible clues. Look for and bag anything—cigarette butts, candy or fast-food wrappers, beer cans—anything that might have prints. I want to know if she was tossed in from here, or if she's up from the bottom after being tossed from a boat."

"Yes, Lieutenant," an officer said.

"A bridge jumper, Lieutenant?" an officer asked.

"Then check any cameras that may be on the bridge or this section of the canal."

"Yes, Lieutenant."

"And I want every house in a two-block perimeter of Sister Street—doors knocked on, people questioned. We need witnesses. Ask about any suspicious behavior in the past twenty-four hours."

"Yes, Lieutenant," an officer said.

"See if anyone had a doorbell camera that might have recorded something."

Larry walked to his car, got in, turned on his ceiling light and scribbled notes on a pad. There was a tap on his window. He opened it. A lady and a young boy were standing there. The lady leaned down.

"Excuse me sir, are you a detective?"

"Lieutenant Chief Detective Gaines, ma'am. How can I help you?"

"Lieutenant, my boy thinks he saw something."

The lady moved the boy to the window.

"What's your name, son?"

"Billy, sir."

Larry lifted his badge and handed it to the boy.

"I'm Chief Detective Gaines, Billy. Hold this for me, will you?"

The boy's eyes lit up.

"Yes sir."

"How old are you, son?"

"Eleven, sir."

"You want to tell me what you saw, Billy?"

"Yes, and I know I did, sir. I saw things tonight."

"Step back, Billy. Let me talk to your mom, son."

Billy stepped back and the lady leaned down.

"Ma'am, are you the boy's momma?"

"Yes, Lieutenant—he's a good kid. He doesn't make things up."

"I'm going to leave this one up to you. You can either jump in the back seat and we talk here or we can meet up at the station and talk there. Either place I'll need you with us as an adult guardian witness."

"Billy, you want to get in a police car?" the mother asked.

Billy smiled.

Larry unlocked the door and the mother and son got in the back seat. Billy leaned over the front seat back, holding the badge for Larry to take. Larry turned sideways.

"You hold it for me while we talk, Billy. Now tell me, son, do you know what a clue is?"

"I think so. Maybe not."

"Clues are like crumbs on a kitchen floor, son. A good detective gets a whisk broom and tries to sweep the crumbs into a pile and see if any of them leads to what actually happened. That make sense to you, Billy?"

"Yes, sir."

"I've got questions—so I'm looking for crumbs—you want to help me?"

"I'll try."

"Billy, you said you saw something. I'm going to ask you some simple questions. That way we can try to put the puzzle together with your answers and they maybe will help solve this case."

"Was that person murdered?" Billy asked.

"Son, let's start with this—do you remember what time it was when you first saw something?"

"It was after my mom went to work."

"Yesterday?"

"Last night, after she called me."

"I work at Fairway restaurant, Lieutenant. I'm a server until they close, and then I help clean the kitchen, usually until midnight."

"So, Billy, your mother called you?"

"Yes, sir."

"I called him at nine o'clock," his mother said.

"Can you remember what you saw?"

"Yes, sir."

"Where were you at the time you saw it?"

""I was sitting on our deck, looking through my telescope."

"Billy loves ships, Chief Detective. He wants to be a ship captain someday. He watches the ships and boats."

"I make models, too. I'm working on an aircraft carrier now," Billy said.

"That's a great hobby, Billy. I tried building a model airplane one time. I was all thumbs with the glue. Is it a modern aircraft carrier, you're working on?"

"I think it's World War Two—I'm not sure. I'll have to look it up."

"Was what you saw through the telescope, or was it with your naked eye, Billy?"

"My telescope."

"Tell me what you saw, Billy."

"I was watching an oil freighter on the Mississippi River. I could tell it was empty. It was riding high up out of the water."

"You have a good eye, son."

"Then I saw two boats come up the canal."

"Two boats together?"

"No. One came up and like, just stopped. It was near Burgundy Street, I think."

"Was it a big boat?"

"Not like a ship. It was a cruiser."

"A cabin cruiser?"

"Yes, a cabin cruiser."

"Can you describe it?"

"A man was driving it. I think it was about forty feet. It was an old boat. It needed fixing up."

"Where was the man who was driving the boat?"

"He was on the top bridge, at the wheel."

"Were the cabin lights on below deck?"

"I didn't see any cabin lights—just fore and aft lights and port and starboard lights."

"You've got a mariner's eye, son."

"Thank you."

"Did it come near the shore?"

"Not at first. It stayed in the middle of the canal."

"And only one person was visible."

"Yes sir."

"Was the man doing anything? Was he talking on his phone? Anything that stood out?"

"He was just sitting—at the wheel."

"Can you describe the man? Was he white? Black? Tall? Short?"

"He was white, but he was sitting down, I couldn't tell if he was tall or short."

"Go on son, you're doing fine."

"Then there was a tri-hull—it looked like it was sixty or seventy feet. It turned into the canal."

"People?"

"There were a bunch of people on it. There was loud music. Some of them were naked—girls."

"How many people, son?"

"I didn't count. Three girls were like naked. I could see that. Their bubbas were showing."

"So, they were like—topless?"

"Yes. They were wearing bottoms. I know one had shorts on and two had like bikini bottoms on."

"Could you get a glance at their faces? Did they look like they were worried?"

"I don't think they looked worried."

"Did they look happy?"

"They were happy. They were dancing."

"Go on, Billy."

"Then that second boat?"

"The tri-hull?"

"Yes, that's when the tri-hull went over to the first boat and was side by side with it and I saw a lady in a dress climb from the tri-hull over to the inboard cruiser."

"She climbed aboard on her own?"

"No. The man who was driving the inboard waved like she was his friend—like he knew her and was expecting her."

"Billy, I'm going to expand a picture on my phone so all you can see is a part of a dress. Can you tell me if this dress matches the dress you saw on that lady climbing onto the boat?"

Larry looked at Billy's mother, requesting approval to show Billy the picture. She nodded yes.

"That's the dress—that's it. That's the lady, I'm sure of it," Billy said.

"Go on, son."

"Is that the dead body?" Billy asked.

"It could be, Billy. Tell me anything you remember."

"That's when I saw the tri-hull turn about and go back to the Mississippi."

"Then what'd you see, son?"

"I was watching the tri-hull go away—I kept my scope on it all the way to the Mississippi. I really liked the tri-hull—did you know they have four bedrooms in them?"

"I knew they would have bedrooms, Billy—wasn't sure how many. How about the other boat, the one with the man and the lady who climbed aboard. Did you see anything happening on that boat?"

"When I looked back at the cruiser he was turning around."

"Could you see the woman who climbed on?"

"No."

"Were the lights on in the cabin?"

"No, the only lights were his port and starboard lights and his dashboard—that was all I saw."

Larry handed his card to Billy's mother.

"Billy, you've been a big help."

"Is the body they found that lady I saw?"

"We'll have to see what the coroner says, Billy. But I want you to know you may have helped us solve a puzzle, and I want to thank you."

"Thank you, Lieutenant," Billy's mother said.

"May I drive you both home?" Larry asked.

"We can walk, It's not far. Thank you again."

Billy handed Larry his badge, crawled out and helped his mother out.

"Billy, did you see any numbers or names on the boats—something that could identify them?"

"No, sir."

Billy's mother leaned down and whispered to Larry.

"He normally would always make a note of names and numbers and times for his ship-log diary, he calls it, Lieutenant. This time he was distracted."

Larry smiled. "I remember being eleven," he said. "He's a good boy. Call me if he thinks of anything else."

"Goodbye, Lieutenant."

Chapter 11

Sasha finished her martini, walked over and set the glass on Charlie's bar. She went back to the table with an afterthought.

"Lily Cup, hon. Drive Gabe to his shotgun and me home."

"Me, why?"

"Put the cigar out, let's go," Sasha said.

"How'd you two get here?" Lily Cup asked.

"Uber. I forgot that's how we came."

"Uber? Where's your car?"

"Bentley's in the shop—and I figured I'd be drinking."

"You need a ride to the shop?"

"Let's just go. We'll talk in the car," Sasha said.

Lily Cup and Sasha, bosom-best buddies since they were both in high chairs. They hiss and scratch like feral alley cats, but heaven help the fool who would get between them.

Michelle Lissette, probably the most successful real estate lady in the Garden District, would "slut up" a couple of nights a week in strapless Givenchy or Chanel that did her buxomly presence proud. "My girls like their nights out," she would say. Michelle incognito would use the name Sasha. Sasha had a fondness for good jazz dancers. Her favorite was currently a black Creole, Gabe Jordan, retired army captain who had served in Korea and Vietnam.

Sasha's best friend, Lily Cup, was her complete opposite—a bubble-butted, bottom of her class at Harvard Law, who had made it through her third attempt at the state law exams. She drank rye neat, smoked cigars, and always won in court. She was conceived on a picnic blanket as her momma's bare bottom rolled in the heat of a passionate embrace and crushed a container of Lily paper cups. Nine months to the day of that picnic, her daddy carried their new baby girl to the bundling table, took the birth certificate and a pen from the attendant nurse and named his new baby girl … Lily Cup.

Sasha and Lily Cup took Gabe's arms and went to the bar.

"Tell me something, Charlie," Lily Cup said.

"If I can I will, my friend," Charlie said.

"Last night when Peck came in …."

"Yes?"

"He came over to the table and he and I danced and we wound up going to my place to spend the night."

"Is there a question buried someplace, bébé?" Charlie asked.

"With all the crap he went through yesterday—and with him knowing Elizabeth was kidnapped in Paris—how come he never said a word about it to me, his best friend. Not one word about any of it, Charlie. What's up with that?"

"That was my doing, Lily Cup."

"You knew what was going on?"

"He told me, yes."

"Why didn't he or you tell me?"

"Well …" Charlie started.

"Whose idea was it not to tell me?"

"In a way, mine, I guess."

"Then fuck you, Charlie."

"I'm sorry, bébé. That's the way I saw it last night after talking with him."

"But why me, Charlie?"

"It wasn't just you, bébé. I suggested he not talk about it to anyone."

"He could have at least talked to me, Charlie. He and I work together, for Christ's sake. Secret things all the time."

"Lily Cup—my friend—last night you came dragging your ass in here bluer than the mold on a stale Danish—you and your main man are now—you know what you two are these days. Last night was about you feeling that loss. You looked empty in your eyes. You were out of gas. The last thing you needed last night was another sad song. You were pounding down rye like you had a murder trial coming up. You haven't been yourself for a week."

"You could tell?" Lily Cup asked.

"Sugar, I'm a fucking bartender. You have a murder trial stone face when you want to shut the world out. When you want to keep jurors from getting bad facial reads. You're known for it. You're famous. Last night you walked in here with tears on your sleeves. You went behind my bar, grabbed a full bottle of rye, a glass and went to a table by the band while they were warming up. I saw you pull the bottle cork out with your teeth."

"I did all that?"

"All that—and then Peck walked in, and he tells me he thinks Elizabeth's been kidnapped, but I can read the man's eyes, bébé—his eyes weren't sure who was kidnapped—Elizabeth, Millie, either of you two, his friends Lily Cup or Sasha or anyone else he knows."

"I'm going to cry. Shut up, Charlie," Lily Cup said.

"You're a sweetheart, Charlie," Sasha said.

"You're a wise man, my brother," Gabe said.

"That's why, and as God is my judge, Peck and I decided together that it was best to try to lift your spirits," Charlie said.

"I woke up hugging my Teddy Bear."

"Who loves you, bébé?"

"All the right people, that's for sure."

"You've got that right, friend."

"Sorry, Charlie," Lily Cup said. "Didn't mean the f'—."

"Never heard it, friend," Charlie said.

"Charlie—not a word to a soul about where Lily Cup and I are off to," Sasha said.

"Roger that. Careful you two—especially about being followed from your place to the airport."

Arm-in-arm with Gabe, Lily Cup and Sasha stepped out of the Blue Note and walked the alley and crossed Frenchman Street to Lily Cup's car without talking.

They climbed in. Then, in a whispering voice while Sasha looked through her purse:

"Lily Cup, you have clients that need you for a week?"

"No."

"You have your credit cards, passport, license on you?"

"Always."

"Start the car."

"Why all the mystery?"

"Give me your cell phone."

Sasha turned Lily Cup's and her iPhones off.

"I know what you're doing, Sasha, but phones can still be tracked, even if they're off," Lily Cup said.

"Just drive."

"Where to, miss bossy pants?"

"First we'll drop Gabe off."

"Then where?"

"Then we'll go to I-10."

Sasha pulled an envelope from her purse. She took out a black fabric pocket satchel.

"What's that?" Lily Cup asked.

"It's a Faraday bag."

Sasha slipped their iPhones into the Faraday bag.

"That bag cuts electric signals, right?" Lily Cup asked.

"That it does. We are now impossible to track."

"Amazing," Lily Cup said.

They pulled up and let Gabe step out. They watched him get to the house door and inside.

"Get on I-10, honey. We're going to Houston Intercontinental," Sasha said.

"Houston? I haven't packed," Lily Cup said.

"My treat. We'll dress in Paris. We're on a nonstop out of Houston at six—a night-owl flight. We'll land in Paris at four a.m. our time—ten a.m. Paris time. Get some sleep on the plane, we're lunching tomorrow at a sidewalk cafe."

"Wait a minute—hold on, girlfriend," Lily Cup said.

"What now?" Sasha asked.

"We only just learned what's going on."

"And?"

"How did you know about needing a Faraday bag?"

"I've always had it in my bag."

"You carry that around always?"

"I use it to cover my garage door opener and my toll road readers when I'm traveling. In it they can't be read or used. I just remembered it—and that I had it here."

"I love it," Lily Cup said.

"Love what?"

"All the cloak and dagger. No fool would know enough to follow us from Gabe's to Houston. If they are trying to follow us they're probably sitting in front of our houses right now, waiting for us to come home."

"I learned from the best, honey. I learned it from Peck."

Lily Cup pulled onto I-10 heading west. Houston's Bush Intercontinental was a few hours away.

Chapter 12

After stacking firewood and getting Baitman Alex's smile and a thumbs up, Aurelie boarded the houseboat and in the cabin where Peck was napping. It had been an hour. She sat on the edge of the feather mattress, and scratched his shoulders.

"What time is it?" Peck asked.

"You slept an hour."

He rubbed his eyes.

"I'm thinking Larry was right, eh bébé?"

"About you needing rest?"

"Ah *oui.*"

"Your mammas is nice, Peck."

"Ah *oui.*"

"She's worried about you—told me she's worried about the look in your eyes."

Peck nodded.

"Mammas knows me, Bébé."

"Peck, what's going through your mind right now?"

"I wish I was in Paris. I could find her and get her safe."

"I'm really amazed at how your mind works, Peck. I can see why you're so popular with Lily Cup and that police detective, Larry. There's something magical about how clear your mind is. It's almost like you can see through people."

"I watch and listen."

"Don't take this wrong, Peck—"

"What, bébé?"

"Like I know there's a lot of really bad things happening and people are in trouble and being threatened and kidnapped—"

"Just, say it. You can say it. We're frien's', bébé."

"This whole thing, Peck—the intrigue—the danger—this houseboat. It all turns me on. Is that bad?"

"Ha!" Peck blurted. "That's adrenalin pumping, bébé. I studied that in night school. You're good."

Aurelie smiled.

"Let's turn the computer on and do some tracking," Peck said.

"Es-tu amoureux d'Elizabeth, Peck?" Aurelie asked. ("Are you in love with Elizabeth, Peck?")

"Elizabeth is my best frien' bébé. We make love, she teaches me things—I would give up my life to save her. I'm not in love with Elizabeth, but I love her. She loves me the same way. Does that make sense?"

Aurelie let a tear roll down her cheek.

"If the computer needs a charge, there's no electricity on Mammas's houseboat."

"It's fully charged, but I can charge it in the pickup."

Peck and Aurelie stepped from the sleeping cabin into the saloon and sat at the table. Mammas and Baitman Alex's lady took folding chairs out to the deck to visit and watch as Baitman Alex prepared his boil.

"What do I look up first, Peck?"

"Dark."

"I don't understand, did you say *dark*?"

"Look up *dark*, bébé. Let's see if there's hidden meanings to the word *dark*."

"So you mean just look up the *word* dark—like you want the definition?"

"Bébé, Elizabeth said in her voice mail message that it was very dark—so, *oui*, let's look up *dark, s'il vous plait*. (if you please.)"

"I have a suggestion."

"Okay."

"Searching *Paris dark* or even searching *dark Paris* might be better, Peck."

"Ah *oui*—dark Paris."

"Here goes ...."

Aurelie did a search for *Paris dark* and the screen lit up immediately with a filled page from the Paris tourism office about all of the "dark" attractions available for tourists in Paris.

"Here's dark activities in Paris, Peck—look at this."

"I see it. It's a whole page."

"What luck," Aurelie said.

"Read them out loud, bébé?"

"Sure. It starts with the catacombs of Paris; then here's the dog cemetery of Paris. This one says human cemeteries in Paris; then here's another one for *Les Egouts* in Paris. That's the sewers of Paris. Here's a picture of it, Peck, take a look."

"What's the first one—how you say—catacombs?"

"That's a place where they buried people."

"Is it underground?"

"Yes."

"I'm not feeling a good clue in it yet—and that picture of the sewer is underground, too, but look at all the lights, bébé. Elizabeth couldn't be there. There're too many lights on."

"I'll try again, Peck."

"Show them again one at a time so I can study them."

"Same ones?"

"Same ones."

"Are you, like, going to put yourself there?"

"Ah *oui*—something like that."

"Okay, here goes. First the catacombs, Peck—long tunnels under the city of Paris filled with skeletons, the bodies and skulls of dead people put there because Paris ran out of cemeteries."

"Closed up now?"

"No, it says here they give tours of the catacombs."

"Hmm. If they give tours in those catacombs, bébé, there will be lights on."

"Probably."

"This picture of a cemetery has big vaults, like in the cemeteries in New Orleans."

"Yes."

"It could be plenty dark inside the vaults."

"Yes."

"Elizabeth could be in one of the vaults," Peck said.

"Could be."

"You know where we are, bébé?"

"Where? What do you mean?"

"We're nowhere. We're stalled."

"I know. It's so frustrating," Aurelie said.

"There's a secret to good tracking."

"A secret?"

"When you stall while tracking, you move on."

"Makes sense. So what's next, Peck?"

"Let's try Gudule, bébé. See if that was a clue."

"How do you spell it?"

"I don't know. Elizabeth just said *Gudule*."

"I remember. Can you let me listen to it again?"

Peck replayed the voice mail.

Aurelie typed out G U D U L E.

"Let's look that up, bébé. Maybe we'll get a clue."

"Wow!"

"What?"

"Peck, it says that *Gudule* is the main character in a French children's book series."

"Maybe we're getting warm," Peck said.

Aurelie turned and looked Peck in the eyes.

"Promise you won't be mad, Peck?"

"Hanh?"

She rubbed her chin in thought. "If I ask something, Peck, you won't be mad?"

"I don't understand."

"I know you know what you're doing, Peck. You do this kind of thing all the time."

"Ax me anything, bébé."

"You said Elizabeth is smart, right?"

"Elizabeth is smart."

"Peck, I remember you telling me one time that when you and she wanted to hook up, long ago when you first met and because she had a boyfriend, she didn't love who worked off shore on a rig that you and she had signals for each other. He didn't love her. They just lived together so she really wasn't cheating on him."

"Ah *oui*. Elizabeth would put a candle light on her mantle if the coast was clear. I didn't have a phone in those days, and I'd walk eleven miles hoping to see a candle light on her mantle. If there wasn't a candle, I'd go to a swamp and catch something to sell or trade for eggs and I'd walk eleven miles back to my shanty in Carencro."

"Peck, when Elizabeth left the phone message, we could hear clearly that there was an echo, remember that?"

"Ah *oui*."

"You read books, Peck."

"I read books. I love my books. What's your point?"

"Do you know what a metaphor is?"

"I know metaphors—similes too."

"What if Elizabeth was sending you a signal by giving you a metaphor as a clue?"

"What are you thinking?"

"She knows how you think, right?"

"Ah *oui*."

"She's watched you track and investigate, right? She's seen you solve crimes, right?"

"Ah *oui*."

"Peck what if the word *dark* was her clue about what tourists think and maybe not about a place?"

"Tell me, Aurelie."

"Elizabeth said *very* dark, right?"

"Ah *oui*."

"Peck what if the 'very dark' she said in her message wasn't a place, but it meant the dark times in Paris when they had so much disease and famine they had to dig the catacomb tunnels underground to put bodies in them."

"So, you're thinking she'd know I'd figure there were lights on in the catacombs place from these pictures and think she couldn't be there but she wants to give me a clue to search, knowing it would say these dark places with number one as the catacombs, and that's where she is, and for me not to get thrown off by the lights in the pictures?"

"Yes. At least that's what I'm thinking, Peck."

"You're smart, Aurelie. What made you think of that?"

"Her candle on the mantle, when you walked eleven miles to be with her. If the candle was lit, that was a signal. If the candle wasn't lit, that was another signal."

"That's good thinking, frien'. Let's keep that idea—and let's figure how a children's book is a clue."

"You mean *Gudule*?"

"Ah *oui*."

"Peck, you're a fisher, right?"

"Ah *oui*."

"If you were hungry and had to be sure you'd catch something, would you use a hook or would you cast a net?"

"I'd cast a net."

"Exactly, so instead of searching *Gudule*, why don't we search *Gudule Paris* and see what comes up?"

"Good thinking."

"Look at this, Peck. There are streets named *Gudule*, *Gudule* book stores, jewelry stores—all named *Gudule*. I don't see much hope for dark places in these sorts of places. Let's look at those children's books with *Gudule* in them."

"Hold on, bébé."

"What?"

"Elizabeth doesn't have a sister."

"I remember you said that."

"I bet that's a clue."

"How?"

"The word sister is the clue—try looking up the word *Gudule* and the word *sister* together like you do."

"I am getting so turned on," Aurelie said.

"What's it say now?"

"It says *Sister Gudule,* prostitute from Rheims."

"Huh? What is Rheims? Is it a place?"

"It's a place in France, Peck."

"What's it got to do with Paris? Could Elizabeth be in a city named Rheims?" Peck asked.

"Hang on. It says here 'Sister Gudule longed for a child but when she had one—Agnes—her baby was spirited away by Gypsies and was a deformed baby'—that's it!"

"That's what?"

"This Sister Gudule is a character in a real famous book, Peck."

"For real?"

"Yes! That's Elizabeth's clue."

"What's the famous book?"

"It's called *The Hunchback of Notre Dame.*"

"Notre Dame, the big church in Paris?" Peck asked.

"That's it. It almost burned down."

"I know that church. Elizabeth told me about it."

Aurelie kept typing.

"Look at this, Peck. Guess what's under the famous Notre Dame Cathedral?"

"The catacombs, bébé?"

"The catacombs! Some of them are, anyway. Apparently they go miles under Paris. I'm thinking Elizabeth's clues are saying that whatever is going on has to do with the Notre Dame Cathedral and the catacombs."

"Because of the dark, Bébé?"

"Because of the book, about a character in the book."

"Could they be holding her in the catacombs?"

"Let me search. See if people live in the catacombs."

"Good idea."

"Look. It says there are illegal parts of the Paris underground tunnels that are unmarked and dangerous, but it says some locals are able to enter the catacombs via secret entrances around Paris."

Peck touched the lid and pushed the tablet closed.

"That's where she is," Peck said.

"Sounds like it."

"Let's not press our luck, bébé. We did good on this tracking. Let's breathe now, talk to Mammas, and we'll eat us some crab with Baitman Alex."

"Peck is Elizabeth a book reader like you?"

"Ah *oui*. Elizabeth loves books. Novels, cookbooks, anything French."

"What if she has that book—*The Hunchback of Notre Dame*—and she's giving you clues from it?" Aurelie asked.

"Tu es plutôt intelligente, Aurélie. Vraiment intelligent." ("You're pretty smart, Aurelie. Real smart.")

"I am so turned on, Peck."

"We've got tonight."

Aurelie grinned. "Ya think?"

"Go see Mammas on deck. I gotta' call Larry."

Peck touched Larry's number on his phone.

"Talk to me," Larry said.

"Elizabeth's in the catacombs, frien'."

"In Paris?"

"Under the Notre Dame Cathedral."

"You're the tracker, Peck. Good feel about this one?"

"That's where she is, Larry. I'll explain later."

"The echoes you told me you heard in her message, Peck, the stations of the cross in the box. It's all beginning to tie together."

"Ah *oui*, like a shoelace."

"As we speak, Officer Downs is in Baton Rouge checking out cabinet makers, trying to find who made the wood box and maybe zero in on some names."

"We've got more tracking to do, but we're taking a break for some crab," Peck said.

"Sasha and Lily Cup will be in Paris by morning."

"They left already?"

"Gone. I'm on a floater case—having the canal dragged for clues as to why a body would have a rope tied around the waist."

"Larry, get Chris or Forensics to look at what kind of knot was tied on that rope. They'll be able to tell if it's a sailor's knot or some paid killer. It'll make a difference where to look."

"The tracker never rests," Larry said.

"I had a long nap," Peck replied.

"I have your passport. How do you want to get it?"

"I've got to text voodoo man tomorrow and tell him. Sometime tomorrow we'll meet up."

"Text him. But if I were you, I'd try to stall him a couple days—buy us some time."

"Ah *oui*."

"And for safety's sake, Peck, I'd leave your cell at home when you venture out to meet with me, unless we meet at Charlie's."

"Good idea."

Peck ended the call.

Chapter 13

The crab boil was a celebration between the combined experienced fishing and cooking savvies of both Peck and Baitman Alex. The friends filled the bowls with cracked crab and set them in the middle of the houseboat table with cups of melted butter, a large wedge of cheese and bottles of wine. Mammas led everyone in a prayer, and the five celebrated the gathering, toasting, honoring, telling anecdotes while picking crab from the shells.

"Mammas, have you ever heard about a book called *The Hunchback of Notre Dame*?" Peck asked.

"I have. In my school days. It was popular, but I never read it. I did see the movie, though. It was frightening and sad. I do remember that. I remember scolding your Mimi for letting me go see the movie without warning me how cruel and sad it was."

"Now I have to read the book, I'm thinkin', Mammas. Next time I come up I'll tell you all about it."

The night ended with Peck walking Baitman Alex to his car and giving him an update of what was going on in Paris. The night was warm, and Mammas was asleep on a cot on the deck. Peck hung mosquito netting on hooks around the deck. Inside he lifted an unfinished bottle of red wine and tipped it back before stepping through the curtain into the sleeping cabin.

The hours floated by and the morning full moon wasn't quite ready to call it a night the next morning when Aurelie first opened her eyes. She was lying on her side with her back to Peck, his arms around her. She looked down her front and saw she still had her bra on. She was in panties as well. She reached around and felt Peck's bare butt cheek and then a gentle clench on a flaccid William. She pulled the blanket up to her neck.

"Morning," Peck said.

"I didn't mean to wake you," Aurelie whispered.

"How late did we stay up, Bébé?"

"I have no clue."

"How much wine did I drink?" Peck asked.

"Enough so you wake up naked and I wake up in my underwear—that's how much. I don't remember going to bed. There were two bottles of red—a bottle of chardonnay on the table and I remember us kissing—oh, we kissed. Who could watch a clock?"

"It was fun, bébé."

"Can Mammas hear us, Peck?"

"*Mais non*, why, bébé?"

"Don't you find me attractive?"

"Ah oui, I always have, bébé, what's wrong?"

Aurelie reached behind her and squeezed Peck's William.

"This. Am I not sexy to you, Peck?"

"Ah bébé, my minds on a million things with all this going on. I'm sorry. Even Larry and Charlie said I'm not myself."

Peck nuzzled her neck and moved his warm hand around her waist onto her stomach.

"I'm sorry, bébé."

Her head melted into his shoulder.

"I didn't bring protection, bébé."

It's all good, Peck. It's all beautiful."

"We could have—"

"Your hugs are the best part—really—I feel wonderful."

"Okay, good."

"Can I do you?" Aurelie asked.

Peck kissed her on the back of the neck.

"I can do you good, Boudreaux."

"Let's sleep some more. I have to text voodoo man at noon. I've got to be thinking what to say."

"I'll make breakfast when we get up," Aurelie said.

"Okay, good, bébé."

Aurelie turned around, removed her bra and panties, stuck them under the pillow, and embraced Peck.

"Now that you know where Elizabeth is, does it mean you'll be going to Paris, Peck?"

"Larry thinks I'm going to be a mule for this voodoo man. I'm not sure where I have to go."

"What do you mean, mule?"

"When somebody carries something illegal across borders for crooks, they're called mules. Sometimes they pay the mules money but sometimes they just kidnap somebody and—how you say—hold them for ransom and make someone who cares about that person be a mule."

"How will you know what you have to do or where you have to go, Peck?"

"When I tell voodoo man that I have my passport."

"When are you going to tell him?"

"At noon, bébé. Let's sleep."

They kissed and both heads sank into the pillow until they were asleep again.

Chapter 14

Peck kept looking at his iPhone for the time. It was nearing noon, and he didn't want to worry anyone by texting voodoo man from the houseboat.

"Mammas, I have to make a call. I'm going to my pickup. I'll come back and we'll eat and say our goodbyes, okay?"

"Promise me you're being careful. Whatever is going on, you'll stay safe, Boudreaux?"

"Mammas, my frien' Elizabeth is in trouble just because she knows me."

"Oh no, what kind of trouble?"

"She's in France, and she's been kidnapped."

"Oh, my God, Boudreaux."

"Don't worry, Mammas. I'm going to save her. I just need time to think. I'll get her back—just say some prayers for Elizabeth."

"Get her, son. Be careful."

"I promise, Mammas."

"He's really careful, Mammas," Aurelie said.

Mammas gave a worried smile

"Peck, can I come with you?" Aurelie asked.

"You can come. We'll be right back, Mammas."

They climbed off the houseboat and into the pickup.

"Are you afraid, Peck?"

"Ah *oui*, I'm scared—for Elizabeth."

Peck texted voodoo man:

"My passport. First prove she's alive."

Voodoo man texted back.

"If you answer her call, you will never see her again. Text me immediately after you get a message."

It was an anxious wait for Peck before voice mail signaled as an incoming call. He waited. When his phone signaled there was a recorded message. He touched the button.

A female voice barked. *"Dites-lui simplement que vous allez bien e t raccrochez !"* ("Just tell him you're okay and hang up!")

In an exaggerated whispering, Elizabeth's voice was loud enough to be heard in the voice mail. Elizabeth asked:

"Elodie, puis-je lui demander de t'envoyer de l'argent pour que tu puisses m'acheter de la nourriture ?" ("Elodie, can I ask him to send money to you so you can buy me some food?")

"Et me mettre dans le pétrin? Dites-lui simplement que vous allez bien et raccrochez. Faites-le maintenant!" ("And get me in trouble? Just tell him you're okay and hang up. Do it now!")

"Boudreaux, s'il te plaît, fais ce qu'ils dissent. Dis à Esmeralda qu'il fait froid comme Janvier 6 seulement double. J'ai froid et faim, mais je vais bien." ("Boudreaux, please do what they say. Tell Esmeralda it feels like January 6 only double. I'm cold and hungry, but I'm okay.")

Peck texted voodoo man.

"I'll have my passport in two days—10 a.m."

Voodoo man responded with a text.

"You will be receiving instructions. Remember them. Follow them."

Peck turned to Aurelie. "She left more clues. Let's go on the houseboat and look them up."

"Give me one now, Peck. I can use my iPhone."

"We already know it's something to do with the Notre Dame Cathedral," Peck started.

"Right."

"And we know it's something to do with the catacombs. Can we try—how you say—search for Esmeralda and Notre Dame at the same time, bébé."

Aurelie tapped the clues into her phone.

"Wow—look at this, Peck."

"What?"

"Esmeralda is a character in *The Hunchback of Notre-Dame.* Says it right here."

"The book?"

"The book."

"That's it, then. That's where she is—under Notre Dame Cathedral. That's what this whole mess is all about somehow," Peck said.

"We need to get a copy of the book, Peck."

"That's where we focus from now on, bébé."

"There's a whole page here, Peck. It says Esmeralda lived in Rheims. Says she was a love child."

"You're right. I have to get the book. It'll be filled with clues," Peck said.

"When we go back to New Orleans, I'll print all this out for you," Aurelie said.

Peck opened his door.

"Peck, you said more clues. What other clues besides the Esmeralda one did you hear?"

"Elizabeth called the woman guarding her *Elodie*."

"Yes, she did."

"That tells me they've talked. That's a clue. Elizabeth asked Elodie for a favor. It could mean they're beginning to become friends—that's a clue. Elizabeth suggested that Elodie ask me to send her money."

"Was that a clue, Peck?"

"Not sure, but because she wasn't cut off by Elodie, just—how you say—admonished, and then Elodie said she would get in trouble. Those might be clues. Those clues tell me Elodie isn't connected with the voodoo man."

"Peck, what if that woman doesn't even know the voodoo man. What if—"

"If that's what Elizabeth is trying to tell us, bébé, it's a good clue. If the Elodie woman is connected to the voodoo man, she wouldn't be saying she could get into trouble. She wouldn't be so careless by letting Elizabeth talk to her during the call."

"What if Elodie is being blackmailed by the voodoo man, too, Peck? Could she be a mule, too?"

"Could be. *Cold and hungry* was a clue, bébé."

"How so?"

"It meant Elizabeth is definitely in the catacombs, because I can tell she's not hungry."

"You can?"

"Her voice was strong. She just added *hungry* to the clue, so Elodie wouldn't suspect the word *cold* was the real clue confirming that the catacombs is where she is."

"You're amazing, Peck. What gave you that clue?"

"I know Elizabeth. She would never say she was hungry. Elizabeth would say she was *famished* or she would say she was *starving*. Elizabeth has a grace all her own. When I stayed with her, we could talk with our eyes."

"Peck, are we staying or going to New Orleans?"

"Going back after lunch, bébé."

"Stay at my place tonight?"

"I have to see some people, but after, I'll stay."

Aurelie leaned over, kissed Peck's cheek.

"You go in and see Mammas, bébé. I've got to call Larry. I'll be right in."

He tapped Larry's number on his phone.

"Talk to me," Larry said.

"I think Elizabeth is in the catacombs near the Notre Dame Cathedral in Paris, and she's okay. I'm thinking she's getting along with her guard—may even be able to get her own way if we play it right. The guard's name is Elodie."

"How in the hell were you able—"

"Larry, you remember the time you and Lily Cup took me to see that stage play with the movie star, Ruta Lee?"

"Steele Magnolias?"

"That's it. Remember when that Ruta Lee whispered things when she was on stage and we could hear her clear in the back?"

"I do. In the theater, Peck, that's called a quiet stage aside, giving the impression she's whispering in secret but loud enough for you to hear."

"That's how Elizabeth whispered when she called. She was pretending I couldn't hear her when she asked her guard a question."

"Elizabeth is smart, Peck. We maybe can work with that."

"Ah *oui*."

"So, Peck—are you saying the guard in Paris, Elodie, might be disconnected from the voodoo man here?"

"Ah *oui*. I'm thinking he could be blackmailing Elodie to hide and hold Elizabeth as hostage. I get a feeling she doesn't know who voodoo man is. Maybe she's reacting to threats or something."

"Elodie being blackmailed?"

"Ah *oui*."

"Like the kidnappings we solved here last year?"

"Ah *oui*."

"Peck, if the voodoo man has been stalking the Cathedral Basilica, he could have been the one stalking in the criminal courts downtown, too."

"That's what I'm thinking, Larry. It's like he has a mule watching over Elizabeth—and she, this Elodie, probably doesn't even know him and can't identify him."

"And so far, you can't identify him, either. Let's keep it that way, Peck. There's no telling what he's capable of doing."

"I know his eyes. I'll never forget those eyes."

"Peck, it's important you tell me the minute you hear from him again—what you have to do for him."

"I will."

"Be safe, my friend," Larry said.

The call ended.

Chapter 15

The Paris taxi stopped at Place Vendôme.

"Oh no, not that hotel," Lily Cup said.

"What's wrong with the best?" Sasha asked.

"The *Aud*?" Lily Cup asked.

"What's with the *Aud*?"

"Rumors have it she was Peter's lover. *Aud* was his pet name for her and it's not the best anymore. These are different times in the world. People are starving," Lily Cup said. *"Chauffeur, gardez le compteur en marche."* ("Driver, keep the meter running.")

"Oui Madame."

"Sasha, it's filled with a bunch of nouveau-riche, stuffed shirts showing off their money while half the world starves. This dump is old news. Staying here would be like staying up all night watching black and white movies. What's wrong with that hotel over there? I want the real Paris, not old movie popcorn among a bunch of assholes who come because it makes them feel important."

"I made reservations. Let's at least have a look and then we can decide," Sasha said.

"Okay, but I'm not into old Hollywood movie sets."

Lily Cup paid the driver and went in the hotel and to the front desk.

"Sir, I have reservations for connecting rooms?"

"Certainly, *Madame*. Let me look for you," the desk clerk said. "Your name?"

"Lissette. Michelle Lissette from New Orleans."

"Thank you, *Madame*."

"I'm not *Madame*. I'm *Mademoiselle*."

The desk clerk smiled condescendingly, "That term is no longer used in France, *Madame*."

Sasha blushed. "C'est vrai?"

"*Oui, c'est vrai, Madame* Lissette. We do have two connecting rooms available. May I hold them for you?"

"You haven't held rooms? I called for reservations?"

"*Madame*, we never hold rooms without a credit card on file."

"May we see the rooms?" Sasha asked.

"Certainly, *Madame*," the desk clerk said.

He rang a bell for a bellman to take them on a tour of the rooms. Back in the lobby, Lily Cup approached the clerk.

"How much are those rooms?" Lily Cup asked.

"$2,047 Euros per room. They come with generous views of Paris. May I hold them for you?"

"How much is "$2,047 times two in US?" Lily Cup asked.

"Excuse me, *Madame*?"

"I can't figure out that dollar, Euro, Franc thing—amuse me," Lily Cup said.

"Certainly, *Madame,* that would be $4,600 US per day."

"That's per day?"

"*Oui, Madame.*"

"Jesus, we don't want to buy condos. We just want to use two rooms for a while," Lily Cup said.

"American humor," the desk clerk said.

"I got it from an old movie—like this hotel—Walter Matthau said it, I think," Lily Cup said.

Sasha leaned over the counter and into the clerk's ear.

"*Monsieur, mon ami et moi avons besoin d'un bain — nous avons besoin d'une sieste—et nous devons aller faire du shopping. Nous n'avons pas besoin d'une plaisanterie de pièges—ne pouvons-nous pas s'il vous plaît être amis, et vous nous donnez nos clés de chambre ou nos cartes ou tout ce que vous avez qui nous laissera entrer dans nos chambres ?"* ("Sir, my friend and I need a bath—we need a nap—and we need to go shopping. We don't need a banter of gotchas. Can't we please be friends, and you give us our room keys or cards or whatever it is you have that will let us in our rooms?")

She patted him on the lapel—a love tap.

"Certainly *Madame,* please forgive my tone. I didn't mean—"

"Stay here if you want, Sasha. I won't," Lily Cup said.

"What? Why not?" Sasha asked.

"I don't care how many movies they shot here or how many movie stars stayed here. I'm not paying greenbacks I could use for Paris shopping for old black and white Paris movie memories that'll keep me up all night with the knocking of Hitler era plumbing."

"I remember Audrey in color," Sasha quipped.

"I want the real Paris. I want today's Paris. Let's find a boutique hotel."

Sasha looked at the desk clerk and shrugged.

"Telle est la vie, mon ami," Sasha said. ("Such is life, my friend.")

The desk clerk looked at Lily Cup and said, "Now perhaps you can buy a red beret for a selfie to send back to America."

With one hand Lily Cup gave him the finger. With the other she handed the bell man a twenty.

"Call a taxi, please?"

The bellman smiled, took the twenty and stepped outside.

They were bagless. The bellman escorted them to a waiting taxi and opened the door. He suggested a boutique hotel they should consider.

"It's more Paris," he said. "It's like Jules Maigret—the real Paris."

The taxi driver waited for them to get in and drove off. They checked in—two separate rooms.

"Are our phones still in that bag?" Lily Cup asked.

"I don't know if it's safe to take them out," Sasha said. "What do you think?"

Lily Cup walked to her hotel room door and waved at Sasha.

"See you anon, honey. Don't make me have to think until I wake up," Lily Cup said. "Jetlag is a bitch."

"I agree. We'll deal with all this later. For now, give me a tub and some rest," Sasha said. "They say it takes a full day for every hour difference in time-zone time."

"Shut up," Lily Cup said. "You're making me have to think."

Chapter 16

In New Orleans, Larry made his way through the morgue into the autopsy room.

"Lieutenant, thanks for coming," Chris said.

"Time with you is always my favorite time, Chris."

"Forensics left a half hour ago, Lieutenant."

"What'd they find?"

"They did their thing on the floater but couldn't hang around to talk with you—had to be at a conference."

Larry stepped over to a side table and poured coffee. He went into Chris's office and leaned against a wall.

"Lieutenant, is there anything new I should know from the meetings at Charlies? Anything to share about what's happening with Elizabeth—that whole nightmare?"

"The ladies are in Paris, Chris," Larry said. "They had a safe trip."

"Both went?"

"Both of them—our coo-coo Pigeon sisters flew all night across the pond and are about to raid Paris shopping."

"God help Paris," Chris said.

"Sasha called me from the hotel."

"Where are they staying?"

"Sasha said Lily Cup wouldn't stay at a prewar hotel. They're in a boutique on the Left Bank."

"I wonder if they'll let Lily Cup smoke her cigars in Paris—or in the hotel," Chris said.

"Not sure, but right now they have bigger problems than smoking cigars, Chris."

"Trouble already? Tell me, Lieutenant."

"I'd say it's more of a paranoia thing than any trouble they've run into, Chris. They even have me second guessing. They're so afraid of being tracked through their cell phones, they have them in a Faraday bag and disconnected."

"Trust Lily Cup to think of everything, Lieutenant. I use Faraday bags for our magnetic building keycards."

"Actually, it was Sasha who came up with a Faraday. She keeps garage openers to her Bentley and Cadillac in it."

"But the ladies are okay?"

"I bought two prepaid cell phones from Amazon France with no names attached and Paris phone numbers. I addressed them to Lily Cup—at their hotel."

"So, the ones you bought are untraceable?"

"Actually no phone's untraceable, Chris. The phone company has to know where your phone is or they couldn't signal your calls. The two I bought are not identified by name, so they can use them without having to look over their shoulders."

"Lieutenant, I'm impressed how everyone is coming together to help Peck and Elizabeth," Chris said.

"That's who we are, Chris. As dark as the hour is, it's heartwarming, for sure. Peck is a brother and a son to us. There isn't anything he wouldn't do to help any of us if our backs were up against a wall like his is now."

"He is a special guy, Lieutenant."

"Now for business at hand, Chris. You called?"

"I did. Thanks again for coming. I'll start at the top, just as you like it, Lieutenant."

Chris held up a large cardboard box.

"How about this for starters, Lieutenant?"

"What's in the gift box, Chris?"

"Lieutenant, I know you have a lot on your mind but—"

"Chris, don't mind-fuck me, what are you hiding?"

"How'd Peck describe voodoo man, Lieutenant?"

"Six-foot tall, almost black eyes … probably hazel green. thin black painted lips, heavy nasal breather."

"How was he dressed, Lieutenant?"

"Open the goddam box, Chris. I've got things to do."

Chris reached into the box and pulled out a headless, five-foot rubber snake.

"Remember wondering what was around her waist, Lieutenant?"

"I do now."

"This is what it was."

"A rubber snake was wrapped around her waist?"

"It was."

"It has no head. What happened to its head?"

"I found rope fibers on the neck of the snake, Lieutenant. The head of this snake was tied by a rope and probably connected to an anchor."

"Any prints?"

"Forensics checked it for prints. Nothing readable. Did your team have any luck with dragging the canal, Lieutenant?"

"This is Louisiana, Chris. The whole frigging state is sliding three inches a year into the gulf. That anchor and rope could be long gone by now. They came up with nothing. City budget wouldn't let them take any more time on it."

"I'm halfway through the autopsy. Step to the table, Lieutenant?"

Larry set his coffee on Chris's desk and followed.

"Do we know who she is?" Larry asked.

"Up until a while ago she was a Jane Doe—"

"Not an easy start, waiting for a missing persons call," Larry said.

"No purse or identity on her," Chris said.

"Damn."

"Lieutenant, Forensics was able to identify her. She's Carissa Rochon. They were waiting on the full FBI report when they had to leave for their conference. I'll have it all in my report to you."

"Cause of death?"

"She died of asphyxia—drowning—body deprived of oxygen as a result of complete submersion in water. Lung and stomach bacterial fluids consistent with the canal water sampling. No signs of struggle, no signs of strangulation or of being bruised in any way. There's no skin under her fingernails from a scuffling. If I had to guess, she was taken to the middle of the canal, the snake tied around her waist and connected to a cement block or something heavy and was pushed in by someone who knew she couldn't swim. They knew she wouldn't be able to think fast enough to unloosen the snake and she'd drown trying."

"Could she have jumped in?" Larry asked.

"I think not, Lieutenant."

"You think it's murder?"

"It certainly wasn't suicide, Lieutenant."

"Is that an opinion, Chris, or a provable fact?"

"My opinion."

"The 'no suicide' theory is not something forensic said?"

"No, that's what I say."

"I've always respected your hunches, Chris."

"Thank you, Lieutenant."

"Let's hear what you've got."

"Carissa Rochon, a seamstress, Lieutenant."

"Chris, the woman had no ID. FBI sent a print report that would only identify her. She had no papers on her and now we somehow know she's a seamstress? Why don't I just shut up and hop on your merry-go-round and listen?"

"She was a seamstress, Lieutenant."

"Are you saying seamstresses aren't suicidal, Chris?"

"Seamstresses live in a world of scissors, razor blades, and the like, Lieutenant. Seamstresses could be far more resourceful in taking their own lives than the horrors of drowning."

"Was there a wedding ring?"

"No wedding ring, no engagement ring, and no ring tan marks, Lieutenant. That's always been a mystery to me— women of her age—and also because Carissa here has given birth—by Cesarian. Scars on lower abdomen. Her ears were once pierced but no longer open."

"Maybe a living son or daughter?"

"That's your department, Lieutenant."

"She's had a child. Are you certain of that, Chris?"

"I am. Is it important?"

"We may have a witness who's seen her daughter."

Chris froze, waiting for Larry to tell what he knows.

"An eleven-year-old sits on the deck with a telescope while his mother is at work."

"Eleven?"

"The kid sees a cabin cruiser come into the canal and stop. Says the only person on the boat was a captain—a driver on the top deck at the wheel. The boat just paused in the canal, and was sitting there, exhaust coming from its tailpipe. A second boat comes into the canal. This one is a tri- hull. This one had loud music playing— a party boat, and on it were topless girls dancing with some dudes."

"Topless girls, and he's eleven?"

"You can see how his attention span might have failed him on picking up valuable clues with him staring at the bouncing titties, Chris?"

"I can."

"But he did see the tri-hull pull up to the side of the cabin cruiser, the captain waving at a woman in a dress and helping her climb out of the tri-hull and board his cruiser."

"A woman in a dress changed boats? What happened next, Lieutenant?"

"Apparently tits."

"What?"

"Our eleven-year-old saw nothing happening on the cruiser by the time he looked. But he did know there were no lights on in the cabin, and the captain was alone when he turned the boat and drove it out of the canal."

"Would an eleven-year-old know a cabin light if he saw one, Lieutenant?"

"This one would. He collects and builds ships and boats. He's a student of the river and canals, like I collected baseball cards when I was eleven."

"He didn't witness foul play?"

"No."

"He couldn't tell if the woman was in the cabin?"

"No.

"Damn."

"What's next, Chris?"

"You said the captain and the woman waved at each other like they were friends."

"Yes—at least like they knew each other. The topless girls were happy and smiling. No visible stress."

"The stomach scars were from giving birth."

"Chris, I've been running in circles on this whole canal floater thing. Let's assume some things in an attempt to get a handle on this whole mess."

"Assume away," Chris said.

"They were having a good time on the tri-hull. They were dancing, laughing."

"And topless, Lieutenant."

"What if one of the dancing girls was the lady in the blue dress's daughter?"

"Or two of them were twin daughters?" Chris asked.

"Spot on, Chris."

Chris held up the bag with the victim's dress in it.

"And what if this was the dress on that 'lady in a dress' that climbed on that boat, Lieutenant?"

"The eleven-year-old didn't see boat names, no boat numbers. Just tits."

Chris opened his laptop. He read his input.

"Lieutenant—Carissa Rochon, Caucasian female, fifty-six-years-old. St. Roch neighborhood in New Orleans, where she rents a one-bedroom apartment in a two-family home, Also rents a small studio behind the house, which is a converted servant's quarter. In the studio, Carissa had a respected alterations business. I'll give you addresses and names for your investigations."

"This is good work, Chris. How did you ID her so fast? Does she have a record?"

"Her prints matched ones on a background check she made to buy a concealed weapon—they took her prints—but this written report says there is no record of her ever having purchased a firearm, although she was approved for one. Apparently she lost interest or need and never bought one."

"Chris, how would you know where Carissa lived, about her studio and that she did alterations?"

"Forensics found scissors and an empty spool of thread in her pocket, Lieutenant. They said those items suggested she was a seamstress."

"My Mamaw always carried a small scissors in her apron pocket, Chris. That didn't make her a seamstress."

"I have more, Lieutenant."

"Sorry. Did forensics tell you where she lived?"

"No, Lieutenant. That was my doing."

"Figured."

"It's a small world, Lieutenant, all things considered, New Orleans is a small town."

Chris pulled three evidence bags out of a plastic file container and set them on the morgue table. He lifted one for Larry to see.

"Forensics found these in one of her pockets."

"The scissors and an empty spool for thread?" Larry asked.

"These scissors may have more *tell* than a common pair of scissors, Lieutenant."

"How? What do you see in them?"

"Note how short they are. Maybe only four inches at best, Lieutenant …."

"Go on."

"And notice the rounded tips rather than the usual pointed tips."

"I see them. They look like beginner's scissors—ones you'd give to a kid," Larry said.

"Or a person who sews for a living, Lieutenant. Someone who might need some scissors on a moment's notice and must carry a pair that won't poke holes in their pocket."

"A seamstress," Larry said. "What's your point, Chris? Like I said, my Mamaw always had a pair like that in her apron pocket—socks with holes, torn shirts."

"As you do in your world of gathering information, Lieutenant, I took the liberty of following a hunch, and I called someone I knew who happened to do freelance alterations for a neighborhood drycleaner. She worked from home and made daily trips to and from the dry cleaner."

"Interesting, Chris."

"Lieutenant, this lady not only knew Carissa. She told me that Carissa worked for years in one of the better hotels in New Orleans as a seamstress. She would embroider guest's initials on pillow cases in the presidential suites."

"Did you let on you were the coroner? Did you tell her Carissa was dead?"

"That's your world, Lieutenant. I'd never step in your turf. My inquiry was more like I was looking for seamstress recommendations—like I was considering Ms. Rochon."

"You're a good man, Chris."

"But I think there may be more to it, Lieutenant."

"Let's hear what you've got."

Chris held up a bag with the dress in it.

"I haven't examined the dress for blood or semen. Forensics felt the shears and empty spool when they cut the dress off. They lifted them out and bagged them separately before bagging the dress and underthings."

"Anything else, my friend?"

"I checked the shears for blood—in case it was used as a defense weapon."

"And—?"

"No blood, Lieutenant."

"Headless rubber snake around her waist," Larry said. "Rope fibers on the neck of the snake. You're pushing a murder scenario, aren't you Chris?"

"And a kill by our voodoo man, Lieutenant."

"I'm buying it, too. You just made my day, Chris. Finally we may be getting somewhere. See you at Charlie's."

"I'll be there, Lieutenant. Thanks for coming."

Larry left the city morgue.

Twenty minutes later Larry was knocking on Billy's door. His mother let him in. Billy was standing there.

"Billy, one question about that cruiser."

"Okay."

"The lady that the captain helped onto the cruiser ....?"

"Yes?"

"Can you remember what she was wearing, Billy?"

"It was a blue dress."

"Was there any black on her dress?"

"No."

"Was she wearing maybe a black belt?"

"No, I'm sure it was just a blue dress."

"What makes you so sure, son? Sometimes our memory can play tricks on us."

"My math teacher has a dress just like her dress. That's how I'm sure."

"Thank you, son."

Chapter 17

Officer Downs called as Larry walked out of Billy's house.

"Talk to me, Downs."

"Lieutenant, can you meet me at the Pontchartrain—coffee and a roll at Silver Whistle? I haven't had breakfast. Just drove in from Baton Rouge and have things to go over."

"It's pushing noon, Downs. What say we meet at the Columns. I'll buy the shrimp and grits."

"I'm on my way, Lieutenant."

While Larry and Officer Downs made their way across St. Charles, Peck and Aurelie were sipping coffee and bidding last-minute farewells to Mammas on her houseboat.

"Mammas, you've lived through worse than what Elizabeth is going through. I promise we'll get her home safe. Just don't ask me too many questions for now. I don't want you worrying."

"What'd you go through, Mammas?" Aurelie asked.

"Next time, Aurelie," Mammas said. "Let's save that for another time."

Mammas handed Aurelie a paper sack.

"Sandwiches for your drive. Nice meeting you."

Peck helped Aurelie off the houseboat then he helped Mammas off.

"Mammas, Audrey told me these people we're dealing with are fools and everything is going to be okay. Aurelie is helping me and believe me, everything will be okay. I promise."

Mammas walked them to the pickup and watched them drive away.

"Mammas is sweet, Peck. You're lucky."

"Mammas doesn't believe in tarot. That's why I didn't want to tell her too much. She thinks it's sacrilegious but she—how you say—respects my judgement, but I don't want her worrying."

"Tu es un bon fils, Peck. Elle t'adore." ("You're a good son, Peck. She adores you.")

Peck and Aurelie were well on their way to New Orleans when Larry and Officer Downs stepped into the Columns Hotel's front room and were seated. The server handed them menus.

"You're looking rather scruffy, Officer Downs. You actually look good with a few days' beard."

"Thank you, Lieutenant. My wife hates the beard."

"How did it go in Baton Rouge?"

"Do you need time with the menu?" the server asked.

"Miss, start us with two beers and two bowls of your famous shrimp and grits," Larry said.

"Yes sir."

"We'll see where we go from there," Larry said.

"Yes sir."

Officer Downs took photos out of an envelope and set them on the table in front of Larry.

"In Plaquemine, Lieutenant, just this side of Baton Rouge, a man by the name of Jack Schneider has a modest woodworking shop in his one-car garage. He doesn't take on big projects, but he likes well-crafted small projects—like building chess board sets and carving chess pieces or wall hanging hat racks."

"He built the box?" Larry asked.

Officer Downs picked up a photo and handed it to Larry.

"Yes, but just the box, Lieutenant."

"What's that mean, Downs—just the box?"

"He's a woodworker, Lieutenant. He made the box, not any of its interior."

"If he can make chess sets and chess pieces, Downs, why would he turn down the whole job? It seems he would have the talent for doing it. Chess pieces and the bottoms of chess boards are felt lined."

"That's what I thought, too, Lieutenant. But he told me nobody asked him to line it or make its interior."

"That's curious. Did they give him a look at what they were building?"

"They gave him a sketch of the bottom and top they wanted—not the interior. He copied it on his chalkboard he has on a wall in his garage, but they kept the sketch. He used the board to write things he'd need to buy, jobs he's working on and dates when they're promised to be ready."

"Think he could identify who came by? Was it a man or a woman?"

"I didn't want to raise suspicion, Lieutenant, asking him that. I was just looking for someone who could build one like it."

"Good thinking."

"Without my prompting, it was Mr. Schneider who offered that he couldn't tell if it was a man or a woman, Lieutenant. He thought it strange the person's head was bandana wrapped. They wore dark sunglasses and black gloves. He also said that whoever it was spoke in whispers. They handed Mr. Schneider five hundred dollars in cash and told him if it was completed within five days there would be a five-hundred-dollar bonus."

"Same person picks it up and pays the other five hundred?"

"That's where it gets shady, Lieutenant."

"How?"

"On the fourth day, Mr. Schneider finds an envelope taped on the outside of his kitchen door. In it was five hundred in cash and a typed note with instructions to leave the completed box outside on the porch in front of the kitchen door. It would be picked up."

"Do we have the envelope, the typed note?"

"Gone, sir."

"No paper trails."

"None, sir."

"Has he spent the money?"

"He deposited it into his wife's savings account."

"Good report, Downs. How'd you get it so soon?"

"Before I went to Baton Rouge I came up with some tactics and my strategy, Lieutenant."

"You a chess player, Downs?"

"I am."

"Let's hear it."

"Doing a sweep, Lieutenant, it's not uncommon for task forces to start in the middle and work their way out. That would mean to start with woodworkers in the heart of Baton Rouge and work out from there. I did the opposite. I wasn't even to the Baton Rouge city limits when I saw a sign for Plaquemine. I pulled off and into a convenience store, looked at my list of possibles and found Mr. Schneider."

"Downs, you should head up our training task force, son. You know how to get things done."

"Thank you, Lieutenant."

"Listening to your report, Downs, you know what's missing?" Larry asked.

"Identifiable witnesses, Lieutenant?"

"That's exactly right, for one. But you know what else stands out bigger than hell?"

"What, Lieutenant?"

"I'm feeling this bandana-shrouded somebody wanted to leave no clues—wanted to be invisible getting in and out. Totally unrecognizable and not trackable."

"Is that a big *tell*, Lieutenant?"

"It's a huge tell. A big, custom-made box gets handmade and slips out of sight with not a soul knowing who's on first or who's on second," Larry said.

"I have another read on it, Lieutenant."

"Go."

"I'm thinking the voodoo man did the same thing I did, looking for a woodworker, Lieutenant."

"Meaning?"

"Meaning if he was from Baton Rouge, he would have started looking for a woodworker in Baton Rouge. My bet is the voodoo man stopping to look in Plaquemine means he's based out of New Orleans and not Baton Rouge."

"Makes sense, Downs. Good work."

"I have a suggestion, if I might, Lieutenant."

"I'm all ears."

"Before we try to analyze what we have or don't have from my find in Plaquemine, why don't we do the same strategy in the world you've been in—in New Orleans?"

"You mean compare notes?" Larry asked.

"Let's hear your world according to Peck and according to Elizabeth, Lieutenant. We'll see if we can back into something that makes sense."

"Peck was at Mammas, Downs. He took a computer-savvy friend to help search clues Elizabeth has been sending. More on that in a minute."

"I had a floater."

"Where, Lieutenant?"

"The canal by Sisters Street."

"Probably a drunk falling in and drowning."

"Why do you think that, Downs?"

"Homicide floaters usually find the Mississippi or gulf, Lieutenant. I know that neighborhood. It doesn't fit the bill for hits. Just my thinking, is all."

"That reminds me," Larry said. "I just thought of something Peck told me."

"What?"

"Peck saw a reader—the tarot lady he swears by in Baton Rouge. She told him this case was dealing with fools and to take them seriously because they could slip up and cause harm, but they would do some very foolish things that would show their hand."

"Talk about the floater, Lieutenant. Maybe there's something you're not seeing."

"The gal we pulled from the canal had scissors in her pocket—small ones with rounded tips."

"Were they in her hand, Lieutenant?"

"In her pocket. She had scissors and an empty spool of thread in her pocket."

"An empty spool of thread?"

"Yes."

"Was it a numbered spool, or did it have a color printed on it, Lieutenant?"

"I don't know, why?"

"Maybe she had the spool in her pocket to know what color thread she had to buy."

"You thinking that's important, Downs?"

"Every morsel is a clue just waiting to be bitten into, Lieutenant. You taught me that in forensics class."

Larry picked up his phone and pressed a number.

"This is Chris, Lieutenant, what can I do you for?"

"Chris, the spool of thread in floater's pocket. Can you tell me if it's, like, serial-numbered, identified in any way."

"Give me a minute, I'll look."

Two sips of coffee and Chris came back on.

"Completely blank, Lieutenant—nothing printed or embossed on it—why?"

"I'm not sure."

"Is it important?" Chris asked.

"Probably not, Chris. Seems every rock we turn we get empty nothings."

"We do know the voodoo man is a killer," Chris said.

"We do know that. I'll be in touch."

Larry ended the call.

"What'd Chris say, Lieutenant?"

"The spool is blank. Nada."

"Flag the waitress, Downs—one more coffee."

Larry did a search for fabric shops in New Orleans. He picked a shop and called it. A shop clerk answered.

"Ma'am, my name is Larry Gaines."

"Hello, Mr. Gaines, how may I help you?"

"I'm chief detective with the New Orleans police, ma'am. I have a question I was hoping you might be able to help me with."

"I'll certainly try, Chief Detective."

"What's your name, ma'am?"

"Darla, everybody calls me Darla."

"Thank you, Darla. Why would a woman have an empty spool of thread in her pocket?"

"I don't understand, Chief Detective. Is that a trick question?"

"No ma'am. I was hoping you might give me a guess—spools and thread being your world, that is. We know this woman's a seamstress—had scissors in her pocket, too, along with the empty spool."

"I'd say she's either saving spools—some folks do, you know. Maybe she just hasn't added it to her collection yet. It could be a reminder she needs thread. Some people keep a spool as a reminder."

"So, what you're saying is an empty spool could be a reminder to go and buy some thread?"

"Not 'some thread' Chief Detective."

"Why not some thread?"

"Chief Detective, an empty spool would be her reminder to replace that empty spool of thread with the same color thread."

"What am I'm missing?" Larry asked.

"Is this lady dead, Chief Detective?"

"Darla, much as I'd like, I can't talk about ongoing investigations, but you could sure help me solve the trouble she's in. I can tell you that much."

"If there's an empty spool in her pocket, there'll be a piece of the thread there, too, Chief Detective. The spool is a simple reminder but the piece of thread is the actual thread she wanted to buy, the exact color and texture of what she wanted to replace."

"God love you, ma'am—Darla—you have no idea how much you've helped. Thank you, thank you. And I just spilled coffee you have me so excited. Thank you so much!"

"Have a blessed day, Chief Detective. Goodbye."

Larry touched Chris on his contacts.

"This is Chris."

"Chris, Downs and I are finished lunch, mopping up coffee. We're setting up a meeting for Charlie's at three o'clock—think you can make it?"

"I'll be there, Lieutenant."

"I need you to do something, Chris."

"Anything, Lieutenant."

"I need you to check the floater's pockets."

"What am I looking for?"

"A single piece of loose thread, Chris."

"You mean a strand of thread?"

"Exactly," Larry said.

Larry ended the call and handed a card to Officer Downs.

"Get the check, Downs. Leave a good tip. I've gotta' towel this coffee off my pants and pee."

"Want me to round up folks to meet at Charlie's, Lieutenant?"

"Good man. I'll pick up Gabe—meet you there. Don't forget to try getting Peck. He should be back by now."

Chapter 18

Peck got water bottles from Aurelie's refrigerator and handed her one.

"Can I charge my phone, bébé? I need to keep it on in case the voodoo man tries to get me."

Aurelie plugged his phone in. She pulled her T-shirt and bra off, dropped her shorts and panties to the floor.

"I need a shower. We'll do more online searching if you want, after."

Peck leaned back on the bed, drinking his water.

"I miss Leah," Peck said.

"Who?"

"Leah Chase from Duckey's. She was a smart lady who could have told me what to do. That woman was about the smartest person in all of New Orleans. Presidents knew her."

"Didn't she die?" Aurelie asked.

"Ah *oui*. I miss her."

A text came on Peck's phone, sitting on the table.

"Tell me what it says, bébé."

He gave Aurelie the access code.

Aurelie picked it up and read it.

"Meeting—three-thirty—Charlie's. Leave phone."

"Get showered and we'll do some tracking."

"Care to join me, Peck?"

"Ah, bébé. Would love to but my brain …."

"What did it mean *leave phone*?"

"So I can't be tracked. I should leave my phone."

While Aurelie was stepping in the shower, Larry was knocking on the door of the young canal witness, Billy, on Sisters Street. His mother opened the door.

"Hi Lieutenant, Is anything wrong?"

"No ma'am. Just trying to tie up loose ends."

"Won't you come in, Lieutenant?"

"Is Billy here?"

"He is."

She turned and shouted down a hallway. "Billy, will you come out here, please?"

The boy came down the hall and Larry handed him his badge to hold.

"Billy—got a minute? I need to button a few things up."

"Hi—sure."

"Why don't you two sit out here. I'll go to my room, catch up on some reading," Billy's mother said.

Larry winked a *thank you* to her. The privacy might let Billy open up more.

"Did you find any more crumbs?" Billy asked.

"Ha! You know, Billy, some days I feel my whole world is dealing with the crumbs."

"You said clues were crumbs, I wasn't talking—"

"I did say that didn't I, Billy?"

"You told me if you swept up enough crumbs, there'd be clues that could help you solve the case."

"Such a memory. You'll make detective someday."

"I will?"

"Billy, let's see if you remember anything else from that night. Can we do that, son?"

"Yes, sir."

"If you're like me, I always remember things I could have said after I get home from somewhere. Does that happen to you, Billy?"

"All the time."

"You go first, son. Do you remember anything from that night that you haven't told me?"

"I told you the three girls on the tri-hull had bikini pants on. Only two of them did. One was naked."

"You put clothes on her for your mother, Billy?"

"Yes, sir. Shorts."

"Were the people on that boat acting peculiar in any way, other than their dancing and drinking?"

"They looked friendly. One of them hugged the lady who got off their boat."

"Did you get a look at her face—the one who hugged the lady?"

"I didn't. Is that important?"

"We think the lady who got on the boat has a son or daughter. Was just thinking the girl who hugged her might have been her daughter."

"Oh."

"And then the tri-hull pulled alongside of the cruiser and the captain waved at her and helped her climb from the tri-hull onto his deck?"

"Yes."

"You didn't see where the lady went from there— after she boarded?"

"No, but I remember the captain handed an envelope to someone on the tri-hull."

"An envelope?"

"I remember it was a white envelope. I couldn't see who he gave it to. It was like an arm that stuck up and the captain just put the envelope in the hand."

"Could you tell if it was a man's or a woman's arm?"

"I couldn't."

"Did the captain speak to anyone?"

"No. The tri-hull just turned about and went back to the Mississippi."

"Billy, you use that term, *turned about*. Can you tell me what it means, son?"

"It's a nautical term, I think. I saw it in a movie when a French naval sailing vessel turned about to attack a ship that was following it. When a boat turns around, the captain will make a U-turn on the water—usually because it has a single screw. When a boat does a turnabout, you can tell it's a double screw or under sail. The captain controls the throttle and rudder and turns the boat in a circle while on the same spot of water."

"Single screw means one propeller, Billy?"

"Yes, sir."

"And the tri-hull did a turnabout?"

"Yes, sir."

"And you watched the girls dance...."

Billy grinned.

"I was eleven once, too, son. I wouldn't have taken my eyes off those girls. Your secret is safe."

Billy smiled.

"Did you get a glimpse of the captain?"

"Which one?"

"The cruiser captain."

"He had a really tall hat."

"A topper. Did it look new, his hat?"

"No, it was ripped and parts of it hanged down."

"Did the captain have a mask on?"

"No, but I could tell he had makeup on, like he was coming from a party or something."

"What kind of makeup do you think it was, Billy?"

"It was like his mouth was black and his glove, I could see his fingers when he handed that envelope to somebody."

"Did you watch him leave, Billy?"

"Yeh, I did. I saw him turn around."

"So, the cruiser didn't do a turnabout, son?"

"No—it did a really wide turn around."

"You know boating, Billy—did the way that captain make a U-turn tell you anything?"

"I remember thinking that it wasn't his boat."

"What made you think that, son?"

"It looked like it wasn't his boat. He wasn't confident the way he drove it and turned around. He could have dragged against anything close to shore. He made a wide U-turn like he didn't know he could damage his prop."

"This has been a big help, Billy."

"Did I give you some good crumbs?"

"You have."

Billy grinned.

"Seen any boats since, Billy?"

"I saw a police boat, but mostly the others I watch are on the Mississippi."

"Thanks, Billy. Thank your mother for me."

"Was that lady murdered?"

"I'm afraid it's looking like she was, son."

Billy's mother came into the room.

"Billy's been a big help, ma'am."

"He's a good boy," Billy's mother said.

"I parked three blocks away. Didn't want to raise any neighborhood suspicions."

"That's thoughtful, Lieutenant. Come any time."

Larry stepped out of the house. He paused and turned.

"Billy, let me ask you something."

"Yes, sir."

"You study boats and ships."

"Yes sir."

"I would imagine—like cars—a boat or a yacht would sort of tell us something about the character of the owner. Do you understand what I'm trying to say, Billy?"

"You mean like somebody getting a Porsche or fancy car or a SUV, sir?"

"Yes, something like that."

"I understand sir."

"You watched this captain do a wide U-turn with the cruiser, son."

"Yes, sir."

"You said it looked like it wasn't his boat."

"Yes, sir."

"As you watched him turn did you have any other thoughts about him, Billy?"

"I thought he either just bought the cruiser and didn't know how to drive it, or he stole it and didn't know how to drive it," Billy said.

Larry smiled at Billy's mother. "Thank you, Billy," he said.

Larry turned and walked away.

As Larry walked to where his car was parked, Peck's iPhone signaled an incoming text message.

"You are on a flight to Paris two days from now—6 p.m.. Be there early—at 3 p.m."

"Prove she's alive."

"Do not answer your phone."

In a short wait Peck's phone rang and a message was recorded. Unlike his other messages, the woman didn't bark orders right away. It was almost as if Elizabeth was talking to the woman (for Peck's benefit) while the woman thought the phone was still ringing.

"Quand ce sera fini, Elodie, puis-je voir votre peniche, peut-être aller faire un tour?" ("When this is over, Elodie, can I see your peniche, maybe go for a ride?")

"Aimez-vous le caviar?" Elodie asked. ("Do you like caviar?")

Elizabeth wisely interrupted the conversation as if telling Elodie that Peck's phone had just answered and it was time to leave a message. Peck heard it all and then he could hear the rehearsed female voice warning.

"Dites-lui simplement que vous allez bien et raccrochez!" ("Just tell him you're okay and hang up!")

"Peck," Elizabeth said. *"When you get to Paris, do what they say, give the man whatever and this will all be over."*

The phone message ended, and Peck texted the voodoo man.

"How will I know what plane I'm going on?"

"When you get to the airport I'll text you the flight number for Paris—a ticket will be waiting. When you land in Paris you tell Customs the box is a gift to the Notre Dame Cathedral from the people of New Orleans, and its only value is sentimental. The combinations to the padlocks will be texted to you. After Customs you go directly to the Pont au Double bridge on the Seine. You stand on it and wait. It will be early in the morning but go there and wait. When you are on the bridge, you'll text me a picture of the Notre Dame Cathedral from it, proving you're there. I'll tell you the code words that will identify the person you give the box to. You will be approached—you will know who to hand the container to—"

"How will I know you'll let her go?" Peck texted.

"When the box is transferred to the receiver, then—and only then—you will be permitted to go find her. She will be very close by."

"Okay."

"I wouldn't try anything funny, Monsieur. This man is very rich and his people would not hesitate to dispatch you from the Left Bank with the fishes of the Seine—and your lady friend would, of course, also disappear."

The texts ended.

Peck copied the entire text and sent it to Larry's iPhone.

Larry texted Lily Cup in Paris.

"Go to the Pont au Double bridge on the Seine. From it take pictures of the Notre Dame Cathedral and text them to Peck. Do it before dawn—early morning."

"K," Lily Cup responded.

Aurelie stepped from the bathroom, wrapped in a towel. Without going into any detail of his latest texts with the voodoo man, Peck caught Aurelie's attention. He was focused and intent on finding and saving Elizabeth. He would not let the voodoo man's texts distract him from that singular mission. He keyed up the voice mail message he had just received from Elizabeth.

"Listen to this, bébé."

Peck played Elizabeth's voice mail message.

"That sounds like it has clues," Aurelie said.

"A lot of clues," Peck said.

"When do you want to do these clues, Peck?"

"I've got to go to Charlie's. When I come back."

"You'll stay tonight?" Aurelie asked.

"Ah *oui*."

"Let me pull some clothes on. Let's try to find these clues so you'll be better ready at your meeting."

"You'd do that, bébé? You're not too tired?"

Aurelie pulled panties and a T-shirt on. She sat at the table and opened her laptop.

"Go," she said.

Peck listened to the message twice.

"Look up the word *peniche*, Bébé."

Aurelie typed and searched.

"It's a city."

"A city?"

"Yes."

"Wait, she said go for a ride. Look up *peniche* and *go for a ride*."

"It's a boat. Sometimes a cruise boat."

"In Paris?"

"Add Paris to that search?"

"Ah *oui*."

"Says here they have a lot of *peniches* in Paris."

"Maybe it's a houseboat, like Mammas's boat."

"Could be. I'll look for pictures later."

"This message shows Elizabeth and this Elodie are becoming close. It shows that somebody has a *peniche*."

"Peck, maybe Elodie is somebody's girlfriend."

"Or mistress?"

"Or that."

"Or slave, like they have here. A sex slave."

"But she said caviar, Peck. She has to be rich."

"Or her master is, bébé. Or maybe he's grooming her."

"What's that mean—grooming?" Aurelie asked.

"When somebody tempts a woman into being a sex slave with money or things—promises."

"What next, Peck?"

"*Give the man whatever*—Elizabeth said it that way. That must mean she knows I'm going to be a mule smuggling something into France."

"That's what it sounded like, Peck."

"Then she said it'll all be over after he pays."

"What does that mean, Peck? She'll let her go?"

"I think it means I'll be carrying something the voodoo man doesn't want to be caught carrying."

"Or identified with," Aurelie said.

"If somebody is going to pay money for it, bébé, why wouldn't voodoo man want to be connected to it? That's the big question. Something's wrong somewhere."

"Who will he pay, Peck—you? Somebody else?"

"That's a good question, too, bébé."

"Maybe the somebody who's going to pay won't be getting what he thinks he's paying for, Peck."

"Dass for true, bébé. That's good tracking."

"What now, Peck?"

"I don't trust Elodie. It sounds like she's trying to—how you say—lure or trap Elizabeth into being a sex slave with her. Caviar—boats. I don't trust her, bébé."

"Do you think Elizabeth knows that?"

Peck shook his head.

"Get some sleep, bébé. I'll be back."

Chapter 19

Larry walked in the morgue and over to a side table to pour coffee. Chris was down on a knee, looking through a file drawer.

"Good, you're here, Lieutenant," Chris said.

"Chris, Peck just got his marching orders, he's got to deliver the box to a mystery man on the Left Bank in Paris."

"Let's go in my office," Chris said.

Chris sat behind the desk, Larry in front.

Chris picked up a property bag and handed it to Larry.

"This is the thread, Lieutenant."

"I'll be goddammed," Larry said. "That gal at the sewing store was right. There was a thread."

"Does the color look familiar, Lieutenant?"

"It looks like *the* color, Chris. It's a match."

"It sure does look like the same color."

"Well, I'll be goddammed," Larry said. "God bless you, Darla, darlin', I think I love you."

"Darla, Lieutenant?"

Larry smiled and gave a wave off, as in *don't ask*.

"Bring it to the meeting at Charlie's, Chris. Let's see if it matches up. We'll save our speculations until we know for sure."

"I think the floater sewed the interior of the box, Lieutenant. And I think voodoo man murdered her."

"What's the motive?" Larry asked.

"That's a mystery. We'll keep scratching."

"The voodoo man kills a seamstress—an interesting stretch, Chris. We've never stumbled into clues this easily before. Sure, it looks like if the thread matches, she could have sewn the box interior. But murder somebody for that? Let's not connect the dots without more facts to back them up."

Larry left the morgue and headed to Gabe's shotgun house.

Chapter 20

A bowl of crawfish sat on the middle of the table as people filed into Charlie's Blue Note. Locksmith Lizzie was first, followed by Officer Downs, Peck, Larry, and Gabe. Charlie set a tray of iced tea on the table and a stack of empty bowls for tails. As each handed the serving spoon to the next, Chris walked in and over to the table.

"Lieutenant, where's the box?" Chris asked.

"Kitchen closet."

Larry took the closet key from Charlie's hand and went to retrieve the box. He came back with it and set it on the table.

"Lizzie, do us the honors please?"

Lizzie had the piece of paper with the combinations in her hand in anticipation. She opened the padlocks and lined them up on the table. Larry opened the top of the box back to its hinges. Chris handed him a bag with the single piece of thread in it. Larry held the thread next to the box's interior.

"It's a perfect match," he said.

Everyone was speechless in anticipation.

"Folks," Larry said. "The coroner and I believe Carissa Rochon used this thread to line the interior of this box. Carissa Rochon unfortunately, could not be with us today to collaborate that fact, as she was found floating in Holy Cross canal by a cop pedaling home on his bicycle."

"Murder?" Peck asked.

"Things may indicate—" Chris started.

"Hell yes, it was murder," Larry said. "Peck, do you remember telling me about a long rubber snake on the arm of that voodoo man bastard?"

"Ah *oui*."

"Our coroner friend here thinks that he tied that rubber snake around Carissa Rochon's waist and tied that to a rope attached to a weight. Then he tossed her in the canal."

"No anchor was found, no rope found, but the snake's head was ripped off, and that's my take on it," Chris said.

"Anybody see anything?" Peck asked.

"An eleven-year-old boy, whose hobby is watching boats through his telescope," Larry said. "He was distracted by a second boat that came in the canal, a tri-hull with topless girls drinking and dancing on deck."

"The boy saw Carissa Rochon climb willingly from the tri-hull onto the cabin cruiser," Chris added.

"Well, there you go," Gabe said.

"Folks, a voodoo man kills a lady who made a living sewing," Larry said. "What's his motive? Why would he kill her?"

"Because she knew what she was sewing?" Lizzie asked. "The lining of his box?"

"Nah-nah," Peck said.

"Murdered for sewing the lining of a box? I don't see it," Chris said.

"What do you see, Peck?" Larry asked.

"He had to kill her, Larry."

"She knew something?" Larry asked.

"She met him. She knew whose face she was sewing it for," Peck said. "She could identify him. She'd be a trail to him."

"I think Peck's right," Officer Downs said.

"Speak up, Downs," Larry said.

"The box was built in Plaquemine, Lieutenant."

"Tell me something I don't know, Downs."

"By a Mr. Schneider and his wife—in his garage."

"And—?"

"Neither Mr. Schneider nor his wife in Plaquemine ever knew what the box was intended for and neither of them ever saw the face of anyone they dealt with while accepting the job and making the box. Mr. Schneider even had to leave it on a side porch to be picked up anonymously. No witnesses in Plaquemine, so there was no reason to kill in Plaquemine."

"Works for me, Downs. Peck, you're next."

"Larry, now we know Elizabeth's in a catacomb under the Notre Dame Cathedral in Paris. We know she's getting close to her—how you say—guard. I'm guessing the guard is so careless, she could be a slave for voodoo man, maybe, but for someone rich in Paris, for sure. She's talking caviar with Elizabeth. We know whoever's behind her kidnapping has a houseboat somewhere—maybe in Paris. We know I have to deliver the box to someone— the Pont au Double bridge on the Seine—but that's all I know. I don't know if I have to wait for money to be paid to someone. I don't know who. And that's all I know so far."

"I read the text, Peck," Larry said. "This is good tracking."

"You were right, Larry. I'm the mule and I fly to Paris in two days."

Two New Orleans police officers came into Charlie's Blue Note's with a dog on a leash. They got as far as the bar and waited. Officer Downs stood up.

"They're here, Lieutenant," Downs said.

"What's up?" Gabe asked.

"Lieutenant, take the box to the bar. The dog will let us know if there are any drugs in it."

"Good thinking, Downs," Larry said.

The dog sniffed the box and indicated there were no drugs. The handlers and the dog left Charlie's.

"The ladies are in Paris," Larry said. "Let me know if we need them for anything."

"Tell them to keep a low profile," Peck said.

"I got them phones with Paris numbers."

"Tell them to have some cash and to be ready to pay for a taxi for Elizabeth, if she gets free. And have them tell us where Elizabeth should take the taxi to," Peck said.

"Got it. Why cash, Peck?"

"If they try to pay a taxi with a credit card—it'd cost time, Larry—time for someone to see them—if they have cash, they can throw it in and get into hiding right away."

"Good thinking."

"Use French bills," Gabe said.

"And tell them not to call her Elizabeth," Peck said.

Larry's speaker squawked.

"Unit nine-eight-four, this is headquarters. What's your position?"

"This is nine-eight-four Frenchman Street. Over."

"Unit nine-eight-four. Body on Magazine Street. Copy?"

Headquarters gave the address.

"Magazine Street—on my way, Over."

"I'll follow you, Lieutenant," Chris said.

Larry pushed his two-way button. "Headquarters, this is nine-eight-four. Coroner O'Sullivan will follow me to the scene."

"Copy that," Headquarters squawked.

Larry and Chris stood up.

"Folks we've got work to do. Let's stay in touch. I feel we're closing in."

"Are you really feeling good, Larry?" Gabe asked.

"I never feel good about kidnapping and murder, my brother, but seeing the caring eyes around this table and knowing the brains behind them makes me feel good."

"Me, too, my brother," Gabe said.

"Peck?" Larry asked. "Can you give Gabe a ride home?"

"Ah *oui*," Peck said.

Chapter 21

The artist's loft was a studio nestled on the third floor of an apartment building between a retail store and a small hotel on Magazine Street. Larry and Chris climbed three flights of narrow stairs. The ceiling was inset with a skylight that filled the room with daylight. Large, heavy, gold-colored, empty picture and painting frames leaned on each other against one wall. An officer was at the door when Larry and Chris got to the landing.

"I have to catch my breath," Larry said.

"Sergeant Hastings, is forensics here?" Chris asked.

"Forensics got here," Sergeant Hastings said.

"What do we have, Hastings?" Larry asked.

"A body in the hallway," Sergeant Hastings replied.

"In this hallway?"

"The hallway inside, sir."

"I take it, it wasn't just a slip in the tub, Sergeant?"

"Female, Lieutenant, fully dressed."

Chris called for a wagon to come take the body to the morgue. He stepped by the officer and into the studio.

"Who discovered the body?" Larry asked.

"We think her dog did, Lieutenant. Seems it kept scratching, trying to get in."

Larry looked at the bottom part of the door. The paw scratches on the wood paneling were deep.

"Looks like the dog scratched for some time."

"Yes, sir. A tenant lady on the first floor had gone out to a hotel bar down Magazine Street and heard the barking. She called it in to animal control. They called us."

"Did she know the dead woman, Sergeant?"

"They only had hallway meets, Lieutenant. They weren't close or friends."

"Thank you, Hastings. Where's the dog?"

"He had a name tag on a thin chain around his neck—Kody. He's in my car. I was thinking of taking him home, Lieutenant."

"I won't tell, Hastings. Kody will have a home."

Larry went inside the studio.

Next to a wall was a tall artist's easel. Clamped in it was a large, heavy golden frame with ornate carvings. There was no picture or painting in it. Against another wall, there was a six-foot long cylindrical machine with metal legs. It was covered with a plastic dustcover. A sleeping bed pushed against a counter that had a coffeemaker and a microwave on it.

"Chris, whatcha got?"

"This woman's been dead forty-eight-hours."

"Cause?"

"Stabbed twice."

"Two times?"

"Both through the back. Hit her heart. No weapon was found. They look like switchblade wounds. A narrow blade, razor sharp by the looks of the cuts."

"Why two times, Chris? She's not a big woman. Why in the back twice?"

"Each entry wound is angled, Lieutenant. My guess is to ensure a kill—the killer wanted to make certain the heart was hit."

"What's it telling you, Chris? Why in the back?"

"Tells me she was doing something and was completely surprised. There are no signs of any struggle."

"Do we know who she is?"

"That's just it, Lieutenant. They didn't take her purse or wallet. It had her driver's license, a bank visa card, and some business cards. She's Nancy Kirkwood. Not married. Well, she's got a divorce pending and a son who's attending Texas A & M."

"Divorce could be motive, Chris."

"Her son is on his way, Lieutenant. He'll be here tomorrow night."

"Who told her son about it?"

Officer Hastings stepped forward.

"He's been calling NOLA police, reporting a concern for his mother," Hastings said. "The calls started two days ago, Lieutenant. He said he spoke with her daily, but when he was unable to connect, he called the police. He was told he had to wait before a missing person's report was good. He said she never once didn't take his daily calls in all the time he's been in Texas."

Larry pointed at the bed.

"Does she live here?"

"She has a home in Covington, Lieutenant."

"I wonder if I know her," Larry said.

"We think she stayed here when she was doing big jobs or was on a deadline, Lieutenant."

"Was she a painter?"

"We found no brushes or oils, Lieutenant. It looks like she was a printer of art and a framer."

Larry pointed at the machine against the wall.

"What is that?"

"Only a guess, sir, but I think it's some kind of printer—only a guess. According to the papers we have on the son's calls on her behalf, she printed pictures, framed them and sold them to stores and galleries. And she would also display and sell them in the French Quarter's art and flea markets."

"Expensive ones? Chris, I'm looking for motives."

Carl, from forensics, pointed at the printing machine.

"If she printed them on that machine, Lieutenant, they weren't expensive. They had to be in the fifty to two-hundred-and-fifty-dollar range. What you'd call impulse art. The kind of art you'd get for your first apartment or so you can say you've been to New Orleans and walked in the

French Quarter. The price of the art would pretty much depend on how expensive the frame was is my guess," Carl from forensics said.

"Any tells of jewelry missing—watches, rings, any tells of drugs—I need motives for a surprise attack homicide. And why was the dog outside. Was it her dog?"

"Maybe the dog knew the attacker and was friendly, Lieutenant," Chris said. "Maybe the victim let the killer in and the killer put the dog out."

"Carl, would you say Ms. Kirkwood here was a law-abiding citizen?"

"It would appear so, sir. Her purse was filled with receipts. Her checkbook entries neatly printed and exact in detail. There was a post-it note that said 'birthday card for Nancy.'"

"A law-abiding citizen's dog has no license, guys. What would you make of that?"

"Maybe the killer left fingerprints on the collar that held the license tag, Lieutenant, Maybe the killer took it off the dog and tossed it," Carl said.

"So, our killer knew the victim and the dog," Larry said.

"Leaning that way, Lieutenant," Carl said.

"Let's find the dog collar, team. Check everything. Check any receptacles on the block," Larry said.

"We'll run prints, Lieutenant. We'll study the place."

"Chris, let me know if there are traces of drugs in her. This could have been a drug deal gone bad."

"I will," Chris said.

"Lieutenant, a bad drug deal is bullets in the face, not a knife in the back," Carl said.

Larry turned about and barked. "I need something to hang my hat on, people. Chris, put this Kirkwood lady in front of anyone you're working on. I need all you can give me on her and let's get back to Charlie's. We've got a time bomb ticking in Paris."

"Yes, Lieutenant," Chris said.

"Hastings?" Larry asked.

Sergeant Hastings stepped in.

"Yes, Lieutenant?"

"Sergeant, I want you to canvas the building. Knock on every door, see if there're witnesses to comings or goings to this studio. Concentrate on the past two weeks."

"Yes sir, Lieutenant."

"What's the dog's name, Hastings?"

"Kody, sir."

"Put a leash on Kody and see if he can find his collar in this building or on the block. We need it for prints."

"Yes sir."

"My guess, Lieutenant, is this murder happened forty-eight hours ago," Chris said. "Two weeks is a bit of a—"

"It may have happened forty-eight hours ago, friend, but for something this cold-blooded and cunning to happen forty-eight hours ago, there had to be a fuse lit long before that. I want to see everything."

Larry turned to the door. "Sergeant Hastings, find out if the stores or hotels on this block of Magazine had cameras pointed in this direction. Get copies of their tapes."

"Yes, sir."

"And give the forensic photographer my number. Tell her to send me what she shoots here today. Overall pictures are best."

"Overall, sir?"

"Wide angle."

"Yes, sir."

As Larry drove from the murder scene on Magazine Street, Peck drove Gabe home and pulled into the drive at their shotgun in the Garden District.

"Peck, are you really headed to Paris in a couple days?" Gabe asked.

"Ah *oui*."

"Son, I know you have a lot on your plate. Can you come in and give me a minute or two? Something I need to say, my brother."

"Sure, Gabe."

Peck told Gabe he was spending the night tracking with Aurelie but was happy to sit with his friend a spell. Gabe put a pot of coffee on and took his seat on the recliner.

"Peck, my brother, I'm an old man."

"You've still got it, my frien'," Peck said. "You're a dancing man at Charlie's. All eyes are on you and Sasha."

"Peck, there's something I want to say—something I need to get off my chest."

"I'm all ears, ol' man."

"My life—and this old soul has been around the horn a time or two—I've been a grunt in a couple bullshit political wars—presidents wasting brother's lives like meatpackers do meat. In all my life, son, I've never met or known anyone like you—someone with your sense of character—who'd sacrifice themselves for a friend before thinking of themself. Never in my life son have I seen grit like the stuff you have in your soul."

"Gabe?" Peck interrupted.

Gabe sat up to listen.

"Gabe, you took me in, a no-account fisher and lawn mower kid from Carencro, and you taught me how to count. You taught me how to read. You taught me how to always think up and not down. How to get my own self into Tulane night school. Ol' man … you are my soul. This isn't me sitting here my frien', this is you. Without you I'd be nowhere—off dead in a swamp someplace."

Gabe interrupted.

"My brother, the day you turned seventeen, I remember it like it was yesterday. I knew Thursday was your mowing day, and I'd go out by the swamp and get my front row seat to watch you go through your routine. I was sitting on a bench behind the hospice, waiting to die—at the edge of that swamp like I always did on Thursdays. It was beautiful. You were one with nature. I'd watch you bait the snood hooks on your trot line and then toss it as far into the swamp as you could. You'd stand there and watch it sink and settle to the bottom. After that you'd cast your net in as big a circle as the wind would allow. That done, I'd watch you start your mower."

A tear rolled down Peck's cheek.

"Son, I remember you looking over at my bench that day—first time ever—you looked me in the eye, smiled, waved at me. and then I remember watching you getting three fishhooks stuck in the fatty part of your palm, the blood covered your hand, dripped from your fingers. I remember thinking what excruciating pain you must have been in."

"Ah *oui*," Peck said.

"Peck, do you remember what you did next?"

"Tears rolled down; Peck lowered his head."

"With your good hand you got a knife out of your pocket and you cut the fishing line the three hooks were attached to. Then you picked up a pair of wire snips and you walked over to where I was sitting on the bench."

"I remember."

"I'm sure you can remember it through your eyes, my brother. but I want you to remember it through my eyes."

"How you mean, Gabe?"

"Son, do you remember the first thing you said? Your first words to me ever?"

"No."

"Standing there with three fishhooks jammed in your palm—bleeding like a stuck pig—remember what the first words out of your mouth were?"

"No."

"You didn't say, you've got hooks in your palm—you didn't say 'can you help me get the hooks out, mister?'"

Pecks eyes closed in tears.

"The first words from your mouth, my brother, were 'Ol' man, you don't look like you want to die here in this place. Do you want to get out?'"

"Seeing your eyes was a sign, Gabe. It was a sign."

"That was you, Peck. That was the Peck we all love. It was that Peck who chose to save my life. Considering my welfare was your first thought, son—not the blood or the hooks in your hand."

"You saved me, Gabe."

"Make me a promise, son."

"Anything, Gabe."

"I don't know what's going down in Paris. It's a scary mess, and I can sense the vibes."

"Ah *oui*," Peck said.

"As bad as this gets—keep your strength and don't kill anyone. Don't throw it all away. My brother."

Peck watched Gabe's eyes.

"Take it from an old black man with slaves in his family, who's had to ride in the back of buses, even in my army early days. Take it from a man who's thought about doing the *thing* every week of his life—I could always justify doing the *thing* in my mind, but I'd think of Mamma, and I'd walk away and keep moving on …."

"I hear you, Gabe."

"No matter how dark the path, son, don't let anybody get you in a hole you'll never climb out of in a lifetime."

"I promise, Gabe. That's a metaphor, right?"

"It's a metaphor, my brother. It surely is. Hee-hee."

Chapter 22

Peck was stretched out on Aurelie's bed. She was at the stove preparing a shrimp *etouffee*, melting butter and toasting an *everything* bagel to be used as a sauce sponge. Peck was immersed, paging through a copy of the book, *The Hunchback of Notre Dame,* Aurelie got from the library. He'd scan and read part of a page, close the book and randomly open it again to another section, scan and read more. It was as if he were standing by a cypress. looking at the whole swamp—learning its culture by watching how low moss hung from the limbs, by studying patterns of lily pads on the surface, watching for breaks in between them for any signs of life and by watching herons drop their beaks in flight, catch a meal and fly off into a morning sun.

Aurelie crawled onto the bed.

"Learning anything, Peck?"

She kissed his shoulder.

"The girl hanged herself, bébé."

"You said Elizabeth is strong, Peck."

"I'm not worried about Elizabeth doing that. She's just passing on clues. She knows I'll never give up studying, tracking, doing whatever I have to do to get her out of there."

"You're in love with her, aren't you, Peck?"

"What are you cooking, bébé?"

"*Etouffee*—waiting on rice to do its thing. You like yellow rice?"

"Ah *oui*."

"Peck with you and Elizabeth, like—well, I mean—does it make you uncomfortable if you and me ....?"

Peck interrupted her, and sat up with a jerk.

"Maybe this is it!" he said.

"What?" Aurelie asked.

"Remember those numbers she gave as clues?"

"Yes."

"At first I was thinking numbers were a combination to a lock, a phone number, maybe an address somewhere."

"I did, too. What are they? Do you know?"

"I still don't know, bébé, but I think Elizabeth has a copy of this *Hunchback* book, and maybe she's finding the clues she's sending me from her book."

"The rice!" Aurelie said. "I'll burn the rice."

She jumped up and went to the stove.

"So, I've been thinkin', bébé. Maybe the numbers she said in the message are page numbers in this book and those pages could hold the clues."

"Peck, I'm going to serve now ...."

"Hokay," Peck said.

"Put the book down and clear your head."

"Hokay," Peck said.

Aurelie turned off the burners and went to the bathroom.

Peck tossed the book on the bed and crawled out.

Aurelie came out wearing a black T-shirt and yellow panties with a smiley face on the backside. She handed Peck a glass of wine.

"Time for a break, Peck. The clues will wait."

"Are you trying to seduce me, bébé?"

"Absolutely. What gave you the clue?"

Peck guffawed.

"Tonight, Peck?" She stuck out her butt with smiley face. "This is your pass."

Peck laughed and lifted his glass in a toast.

"Aurelie, thanks for being my frien', helping me try to—how you say—unravel this mess."

"You'd do it for me. Besides, you're the best Zydeco dancer I know. I don't want to lose that."

"Ha!"

While Peck and Aurelie sat for dinner, Larry was calling Lily Cup's phone in Paris.

"*Bon jour*?" Lily Cup said.

"What time is it there, girl?" Larry asked.

"It's one a.m. here in Paris," Lily Cup said. "I can't sleep. Reading case notes on a witness deposition I have when I get back. How are you sweety? How're the boys? Are you calling me from home or the station?"

"My two boys are terrific. Both seem to be in a track and field state of mind. Let's see where they go with it."

"No daddy pressure," Lily Cup said.

"Just encouragement. When I was young, no one— neither my dad or mom—made me play basketball," Larry said.

"Why so late, Larry? What's on your mind?"

"I just came from a meeting with forensics. We have a murdered female, and the only evidence we have is she was stabbed in the back. Can't find a motive for homicide—and we can't find any witnesses. Nothing in her studio was worth over a couple hundred bucks."

"Any evidence they took money, Larry?"

"Never touched her purse."

"What'd Peck say?"

"Peck hasn't seen the scene. He's studying Paris— on a friend's computer," Larry said.

"From what you've told me, Larry, I can guess what Peck would say."

"And what would our friend say?"

"Peck would say the only reason you find no clues is because the murderer wanted you to know you didn't find any."

"Wants us to know we're outsmarted?" Larry asked.

"That's my take on it," Lily Cup said.

"I'm thinking that, too."

"Peck would say if a scene has been wiped this clean it would be more than a premeditated hit—it would have been coming to a scene to remove more evidence than the hit," Lily Cup said. "Something else was going down."

"Like a last wipe-down," Larry said.

"Exactly. Trick is to try to figure out if she wasn't there when he came to wipe, would he have still killed her."

"We think the murderer knew the dog—let it out—maybe removed the dog's collar," Larry said.

"There you go, Larry."

"So, the murderer came back to mop up evidence, and the lady with two stab wounds in her back was part of the mopping up?" Larry asked.

"She was the evidence, Larry. She knew something he didn't want anyone to know."

"Why wouldn't he kill the dog, too? Why just take the collar and lock the dog outside?" Larry asked.

"Because the killer is arrogant, Larry. He wanted you to know he's pulled one over on you."

"You think?" Larry asked.

"Either that, or he's a fool," Larry.

"I'll buy that."

"Larry, I remember a criminal law class at Harvard. My professor had us go out, we had to find and introduce ourselves to someone—anyone—involved in criminal law. Police, attorneys, jailers even—buy them a drink or a cup of coffee and interview them."

"Which way did you go?"

"Before I looked for someone, I read a couple of mystery novels to guide me, and I wound up connecting with a retired Irish undercover cop in Boston. The *French Connection* type dude. He trusted me because I drank rye straight up and we both smoked cigars. He was big time in the underworld, but you would never know it watching him walk around or sitting at a bar. He was famous for some of Boston's biggest busts—cracking cases and never once being seen at the scene, on television news or in the newspapers. He never blew his cover."

"I'm liking it so far," Larry said.

"I asked him if he was only permitted to tell me one thing that would help me in law—one piece of advice— what would it be?"

"What'd he say?"

"He told me that on Mafia hits—almost always, the shooter would lay the weapon on the body or on a table next to the body and leave."

"Yes!" Larry said. "Did he tell you why?"

"He told me that at a murder scene, the team— police, detectives, forensics, photographer, the coroner—all come in like they're in a movie and they all jump in the same rowboat like they're a rowing team, thinking in unison—"

"Yes."

"First thing shouted is, 'find the weapon.'"

"Yes."

"But with the weapon sitting on the victim's chest or next to the body, it's a wrinkle, and it throws the rowers in the boat off kilter."

"It'd totally distract them," Larry said.

"Exactly, Larry."

"That's when Columbo sends for coffee," Larry said.

"Ha! You got it! Larry, I miss you so much."

"Good story. I needed that."

"My guess, big guy—?" Lily Cup started.

"What's your guess, sweety?"

"How many rooms are there at the scene?"

"One large studio—glass ceiling, one bathroom, short hall between studio and bathroom."

"Let Peck look at it, Larry."

"Anything else?"

"My guess is the big clue is still in the room, Larry."

"How'd you come up with that?"

"Sherlock Holmes always said the best place to hide something where no one will find it is right in front of them."

"If he did a wipe, why would he be hiding anything?"

"Because he's an arrogant sonofabitch, Larry."

"I'll be—" Larry started.

"Miss you, punkin.' Get Peck to look at the room."

"I'll call you tomorrow," Larry said.

Larry ended the call and texted Peck's phone.

"Charlie's ten a.m. Things to talk about."

Peck responded.

"K"

"Leave your phone behind," Larry texted.

Peck responded.

"Are we going to a station or the morgue?"

"No—just Charlie's."

"Then I can bring my phone. I need it with me."

Larry didn't respond.

"Who was that?" Aurelie asked.

"Larry needs me in the morning."

"Are you still staying tonight?"

"Ah *oui.*"

"Did I overcook the shrimp?"

"Shrimp—three minutes, perfect, bébé."

Aurelie grinned.

"Peck, look at the pages for those numbers like you were talking. See if you can find any clues. I'll pick up the kitchen."

"I can help," Peck said.

"You do the tracking. See what you can find. I want you all to myself after that."

Peck smiled, stepped over to the bed, plopped down, picked up the book, and cracked it open. He turned his iPhone on and played Elizabeth's voice mail several times. He set his phone down and turned to a page of the book. He read it from top to bottom.

"Listen to this, bébé."

Peck read a section from the book aloud.

"It is the day three hundred and forty-eight years six months and nineteen days since the good people of Paris were awakened by a grand peal from all the bells in the three districts of the City, the University and the Ville."

"What's that mean to you, Peck?"

"I'm convinced of her having the book. Elizabeth always takes books when she travels. I think it means she probably has *The Hunchback of Notre Dame* with her. She's read about France—going there. They probably let her keep it to keep her quiet."

"And she's reading it, looking for clues to send you."

"Exactly, bébé. She is smart. Her first clues told us, we just didn't pick up on it for a while."

"You're smart, Peck—figuring out the page number thing—is it working?"

"I think so."

"That thing you just read, what's it mean?"

"She gave me the numbers so I would look up those page numbers. She wanted me to read that part of the book."

"What's the part you read tell you?" Aurelie asked.

"It tells me—people of Paris woke up to a grand peal from all the bells—I think that means every bell in Paris was ringing but that was more than a hundred years ago, so I'm thinking her clue is that this whole kidnap thing and me carrying the box thing has something to do with the

Notre Dame Cathedral burning down—'dass for true—I know it now. Bells rang all around the world while the whole world watched the fire for a week."

"Everything stopped, Peck."

"My frien' Gabe and I watched it at Sasha's house."

"People donated billions to the cathedral in just days, Peck."

"Ah *oui*. And a billion each from rich people who can donate that kind of money draws sludge bottom feeders like hurricanes draw street pirates," Peck said.

"And she's under that cathedral, right?"

Peck rested back.

"Let's find January 6. Remember that clue, Bébé?"

Aurelie tapped in *The Hunchback of Notre Dame* and January 6. Some paragraphs appeared on the screen.

"Peck, read this—"

'What set in motion all the population of Paris on the 6th of January was the double solemnity, united from time immemorial, of the epiphany and the Festival of Fools.'

"That's it."

"What's it?"

"That's what I've been looking for," Peck said.

"What?"

"Audrey was right, bébé. I'm dealing with fools."

"Listen to this, Peck."

"On that day there was to be an exhibition of fireworks—" Aurelie said. "I bet that's the way she's telling us it's all about the Notre Dame burning."

"There has to be a reason she's under the cathedral," Peck said.

Peck turned pages, trying to put the puzzle together.

When morning came, they were both sound asleep with all the lights on. Aurelie still in her T-shirt and yellow panties, Peck fully dressed. By the time Peck awakened, Aurelie had gone to work.

Chapter 23

Peck drove to Magazine Street, parked and climbed the three flights of stairs to find Larry and Officer Downs in the crime scene studio.

"Larry, Jason, how you all are?"

"Glad you could come, Peck," Larry said. "Need to borrow your eyes for a look-see, and then we'll go to Charlie's and try to unravel that mess."

Peck scanned the studio as if it were a swamp and he a predator looking for prey—the sun's reflection off an eye, a sudden movement, something that didn't fit.

"The victim's son is on his way, Peck. He should be here any minute."

"What happened, Larry?"

"Female, Nancy Kirkwood, knifed twice in the back. No sign of struggle, no prints anywhere—not even hers. Which leads us to believe the place had been wiped, no witnesses, nothing of value in the place to be taken, no evidence of anything being taken."

"Any signs of money? Drugs?" Peck asked.

"Her purse wasn't touched. Intact. License, credit cards, receipts, business cards—all there."

"You said her prints weren't anywhere, Larry. Not even on her purse?"

"Her prints *were* on her purse, Peck. Sorry."

"No witnesses?"

"A dog was outside, scratching to get in."

"The corpse's dog?"

"We're assuming so. Damn near scratched through the door trying to get in."

"Anybody see that happening—the dog scratching?" Peck asked.

"I saw the dog scratching when I first got here," Downs said. "CSI went in through the fire escape window. We think the killer took the dog's collar, fingerprints. We think the killer knew the dog and put him out before killing the Kirkwood lady."

"Is the dog at the pound?"

"Sergeant Hastings has him at home, Peck," Downs said. "Kody. Hastings is prepared to give the dog up if a legitimate owner steps forward."

"If we have a suspect lineup, maybe the dog—Kody—will identify someone," Peck said.

"Weapon?" he asked.

"Peck, Chris said it was razor-sharp—a switch blade. Twice in the back at angles that ensured hitting the heart."

"This doesn't sound like a—how you say—impulse murder of passion, like, jealousy or rage," Peck said.

"I'm impressed, Peck. Agree, but seeing nothing—"

"Something's gnawing on me, Larry," Peck said.

"Let it out."

"This was an assassination, Larry."

"You think?

"Ah *oui*."

"A professional hit?"

"My gut's tellin' me she knew too much, Larry."

"What are you thinking she knew too much of?"

"Stabbed in the back, Larry—a sneak attack. She couldn't see it coming."

"What's that saying to you, Peck?"

"I don't think she knew what she knew could get her killed."

A man appeared at the studio door.

"Who's in charge here?" he asked.

Larry walked over, extending his hand.

"I'm Chief Detective Gaines. And you are?"

"I'm Doyle Kirkwood."

"Mr. Kirkwood."

"This is my mother's studio."

"We're sorry for your loss, Mr. Kirkwood," Larry said. "We're hoping you may be able to help us find who did this to your mother."

"Thank you, Chief Detective—call me Doyle—but I must tell you I'm not pleased with you right now—well, with New Orleans."

"I'm sorry." Larry said.

"I tried to tell the police something was wrong with Mother days ago, but I couldn't get anyone's ear. I called from school in Texas."

"I understand you tried, Doyle, and I'm sorry for a system that is so inflexible it requires a certain length of time to pass before a person can be listed as missing—"

Pointing at the easel, Doyle interrupted Larry.

"Chief Detective—?"

"Yes?"

"Mother was robbed."

"You know this, or are you guessing, son."

"Somebody murdered and robbed my mother."

He began crying.

Peck motioned for Larry and Downs to stay back as he stepped over and put his arm around Doyle's shoulder.

"Doyle—I'm Peck—and my mammas was raped in a mental hospital men's room when she was nineteen visiting her mammas in the hospital."

"Why are you telling me this?" Doyle asked.

"That man who raped Mammas became my father. It took some time, but a nice old man was fishing with that man one day and found out what the man had done to my mammas and two other girls at the hospital, and the nice old man shot him in the face with a shotgun—left him to rot for gators."

Doyle tried to push Peck away. Why are you telling me this?"

"I'm telling you because if I was there at that time, I would have shot that man who raped my Mammas even if he was my father. I promise you, frien'—we won't rest until this person pays for what he did to your momma. I promise."

"Mother never knew a stranger," Doyle said. "She was fun-loving. She worked hard putting me through school. We spoke every day—like clockwork. It was my way of saying *I love you* and watching over her."

"You're a good son," Peck said. "She was proud."

"Doyle, you said she was robbed," Larry said.

"She was," Doyle said.

Doyle pointed at the gold frame on the easel stand.

"Explain that, son. It's an empty frame."

"No, it isn't, Chief Detective."

Doyle stepped to the easel. "Can I touch it, Chief Detective?"

"Yes—go ahead, son."

Doyle lifted the large golden frame from the easel, turned it around and pointed to the inner edge behind the frame.

"See this frame connected behind this big ornate gold frame, Chief Detective?"

"I see it—go on."

"That wood frame is for a painting to be attached to it, Chief Lieutenant. Somebody cut the painting out of this frame," Doyle said.

Larry touched numbers on his phone.

"CSI?" a voice answered.

"Goddammit, I need forensics on Magazine Street and I want them here pronto."

"Who is this?"

"Chief Detective Larry Gaines."

"Lieutenant, forensics is at a burglary scene."

"Well, this is a murder scene, and I want them here now to finish your job."

"The studio on Magazine Street, Lieutenant?"

"That's the one."

"That studio was scoured thoroughly, Lieutenant—we went over it for two days. Why the urgency?"

"Because the place wasn't scoured," Larry said. "I love your team but someone walks in from Texas and in two minutes finds material evidence that was here when you were here, and motive, staring us in the face."

"They're on their way, Lieutenant."

Larry ended the call.

"Forensics will be here. You're observant, Doyle. You may have helped us find your mother's killer."

"Mother and I did Facetime every day at the same time, Chief Detective."

He opened his iPhone and showed Larry a picture of his mother standing in front of the easel and talking to him.

"See the frame behind my mother?"

"I do, son."

The picture showed a large gold frame attached to the easel with an oil painting of a sailing ship in a storm.

"The painting's gone. Mother was robbed."

"When did you take that cell phone picture, Doyle?"

"Four days ago, when we did our Facetime. Three days ago was the first time she didn't answer and that's when I called the police. They told me I had to wait."

"Is that an expensive painting?" Larry asked.

"I don't know anything about art, Chief Lieutenant."

"Doyle, will you text me the picture?"

Doyle obliged.

"I wonder what the painting's worth," Larry said.

"Very little, Chief Detective."

"You can tell? You said you didn't know art?"

"It's just a print—not worth murdering someone for. Mother could barely pay the rent here."

"Interesting."

"Last year someone convinced Mother that getting that inkjet printer over there against the wall would make her a lot of money. That's why she leased this studio—to be closer to stores and markets."

"I understand, son."

"We have a place in Covington, but Mother didn't like having to drive in every day. She'd stay here a few days at a time—on that bed."

"It hadn't paid off—the machine, Doyle?"

"Every photo shop and pharmacy in the state has one just like it. She was sold a pipe dream that never happened."

Doyle began to weep.

"She probably owed the wrong people money and they killed her for it."

"We need to identify the body—you up to it today?"

"Can I make funeral arrangements and see Mother tomorrow, Chief Detective?"

"Yes, of course, take your time. Give me your contact information. Call me on the line you just texted when you're available."

"I will. Thank you, Chief Detective."

"I have a question, Doyle," Peck said.

"Okay."

"Pictures are just pictures, aren't they?"

"I don't understand the question."

"Photographs—some are printed in color and some are in—how you say—black and white, right?"

"Yes."

"But they are all prints, right?"

"Yes—prints."

Peck pointed at the machine against the wall.

"When I fish, I always use my best snoods and clean hooks. When I throw a net, I have a favorite, what I think is a 'lucky' casting net."

"What's your point?" Doyle queried.

"Doyle, what is it about that machine over there that made your momma think she should borrow money to buy it, spend a lot more money to rent this studio and by buying the machine and renting the studio it would make her a lot of money?"

"Giclee."

"Say that again?" Peck asked.

"They sold her a bill of goods on giclee—that inkjet printer prints giclee."

"What does giclee mean?" Peck asked.

"Giclee prints a heavy inkjet—as Mom explained it to me, it's a dissolve and printing—an ink applying process."

"I don't understand, Doyle. Don't all—how you say—photograph printers print the same?"

"Not all printers print on canvas."

"On canvas?"

"Yes—not all printers print on canvas," Doyle said. "That machine does."

"I think I understand. Can you tell me why your momma would think that would make her a lot of money?"

"What it prints, looks and feels like real oil paintings on canvas, but they're only giclee prints, printed on canvas, stretched on a frame just like oil paintings. But they're not oil paintings," Doyle said. "Now do you understand?"

"Ah *oui*."

"Giclees cost more than prints on paper, because they look valuable on canvas, but they're not expensive."

"Any more questions, Peck?" Larry asked.

"No—not now. Thank you, Doyle. Sorry about your momma. She's watching over you. I promise we'll solve this case."

"Thank you."

"Thanks for coming, Doyle," Larry said. "Call me."

"Yes, Chief Detective. Please find whoever did this to my mother."

"Peck?" Larry asked.

"Yes?"

"Go on ahead to Charlie's. I'll be along."

"Hokay."

"Downs, hang here until Forensics come, let them in and then head on over to Charlie's."

"Yes, Lieutenant."

On his way to Charlie's Blue Note, Larry stopped at a famous local art museum. The curator wasn't in.

"Ma'am, I'm Lieutenant Gaines with New Orleans Police. I need Helio to take a look at something for me. Can you show him when he comes in—ask him to give me a call?"

"I'll be happy to, Lieutenant."

She gave Larry their email address. He sent the picture to the email address. He started to leave.

"Helio should be here any minute, Lieutenant, would you care to wait? We have coffee."

"Thanks, ma'am. I've got to get to a meeting on a case we're working on or I would."

"Does what you need from Helio have anything to do with the case you'll be meeting on?"

"That's just it—not sure. We're trying to solve a murder and looking under every rock. Just tell Helio I'll be in a meeting at Charlie's Blue Note."

"I understand, Lieutenant. I'll give it to Helio right away and tell him how important it is."

"Thank you, ma'am."

"Will Charlie be in the meeting, Lieutenant?"

"He will. You know Charlie?"

"Tell Charlie Dawn says hello."

"I will indeed."

"Thank you."

"Helio may want to keep this confidential," Larry said.

"I understand, Lieutenant."

On the way to his car Larry touched contact on his phone for Officer Downs.

"Lieutenant?" Downs asked.

"Downs, will the easel fit in your car?"

"What do you have in mind, Lieutenant?"

"My guts telling me I want the easel and that frame at Charlie's for our meeting. Don't ask me why."

"I'll arrange portage, Lieutenant. I'll figure it out."

"I was sure you would, Downs. See you at Charlie's. If forensics puts up a stink, have them call me."

"Yes, sir."

Chapter 24

Peck remembered a throwaway cell phone in his pickup's console. He checked its charge and pulled over in front of the alley to Charlie's Blue Note and parked. With his regular iPhone he searched the number to the phone store on Canal Street. He tapped numbers in, eventually got Aurelie on the phone.

"I fell asleep last night, bébé—so sorry."

"We both fell asleep, Peck. Oh well, we'll always have Zydeco."

"Ah *oui*."

"Is that why you called? To apologize for sleeping?"

"Nah-nah."

"What's up?

"Bébé, you remember how you could look up—how you say—information about who calls who, like that?"

"Je n'aime pas en parler au téléphone, mais oui, qu'en est-il?" ("I don't like talking about it on the phone, but yes, what about it?")

"I need really smart people with working the phone things—like the tricks they do at this meeting I'm going to."

"My boss, Ronda, is a wizard with phones. That's why she's the boss."

"Can Ronda be trusted?"

"You met her. I've known her a long time. She's totally trustworthy. She'd do anything to help."

"That's so good. Are you sure though, bébé?"

"Peck, I have a confession."

"Uh-oh—what?"

"I told Ronda about those girls you helped. You know, the ones who were being used as sex slaves."

"Ah *oui*."

"Well when you needed help trying to find out who was kidnapping and killing those people that time, I told Ronda about it and she offered to help me—even showed me how to do it."

"*Aye yi-yi*!"

"Do you hate me, Peck?"

"No way. Can you get her to meet with us at Charlie's Blue Note, bébé? You come, too. We've got to bring all the brains we can. Time's running out for Elizabeth. I don't feel good about where we are. It's all still in the dark."

"When's the meeting?"

"I'm in front of Charlie's now, but with everything on my mind, I forgot my frien' Gabe, so I'll go get him and then come back here."

"*Ne bouge pas un muscle, Peck. Je vais voir ce que dit Ronda.*" ("Don't move a muscle, Peck. I'll go see what Ronda says.")

Peck had driven up the drive to his and Gabe's shotgun house when Aurelie came back on the phone.

"Are you still there, Peck?"

"Ah *oui*."

"We'll be at Charlie's. What time?"

"Gabe and I will be heading there in a few minutes, bébé? She's really coming? Ronda?"

"She's coming and she's smart. You'll be glad she came," Aurelie said.

Chapter 25

Peck used his throwaway phone to call Larry.

Larry answered.

"Who's calling?"

"Me," Peck said.

"Talk to me."

"I've got Gabe. We're on our way. I need you to text a number for Sasha or Lily Cup in Paris."

"Either?"

"Lily Cup, I'm thinkin'."

A text came with Lily Cup's number in Paris.

"What's going on, my brother?" Gabe asked.

"Gabe, you ever watch a fish turn and jump so many times loops of fishing line start to curl around the tip of your rod?"

"My army days. It was in Jersey. Me and brothers would go over to the Delaware river during the spring run and rent an old row boat—pay too much to an old black brother, a school janitor in New Hope. He'd trailer it to the river and set it on the Delaware for us, sit and wait all day while we fished. For another five bucks he'd throw in an outboard motor. We couldn't afford gas for it, so we'd take turns rowing."

"Gabe, you remember the time I was in jail up there in Trenton and that cop slugged me in the stomach because I talked funny?"

"I'll never forget your stories, son."

"That's the feeling in my gut now. I'm scared."

"My brother."

"And I don't hardly ever get scared."

"Peck, I had to learn how to grow up scared in the day my own momma couldn't eat in restaurants. Had to sit in the back of busses and earned dirt pay for shit work. But you know what, my brother?"

"What?"

"If I ever looked down and not up—if I ever complained about my lot—if I ever looked envious at the white world passing me by—my momma would slap me side the head so hard I could count stars."

Peck smiled.

"Peck, life ain't what you don't have."

"No?"

"Life is what you do have. You're wasting time worrying about what you don't know and about what's going on in Paris. Am I right, son?"

"Ah *oui*."

"Well count what you do know—and if you're making yourself keep from doing something because you're afraid of the dark, you're letting those bastards behind all this bullshit write the rules. You write the rules, son. Do what my daddy always taught me."

"What's that, Gabe?"

"My daddy would say 'If a big dog runs at you, whistle for it!'"

"Ha!"

Peck pulled to the curb in front of Charlie's. They got out and hugged.

"Let's do it," Peck said. "Let's whistle."

"My brother," Gabe said.

Chapter 26

Charlie had pushed tables together to arrange things like a conference table. An iPad tablet rested on a cookbook stand from the kitchen. The idea was to include Sasha and Lily Cup live from Paris, via FaceTime.

Peck wasn't alone with his tension brought on by anxiety. Each person who came for the meeting was solemn-faced. Peck and Gabe were first. Locksmith Lizzie from forensics was next. Officer Jason Downs carried in the artist's easel and the attached gold frame and set it a few feet from the table. The coroner, Chris O'Sullivan was next. Chief Detective Larry Gaines was next. Peck's friend, Aurelie, and Ronda, the manager of the phone store, walked in and took seats. Peck introduced them to everyone.

As people settled around the table, there was a knock on the door. It was Helio, the curator from the art museum. Charlie invited him in and introduced him around. Helio walked over to the artist's easel, put reading glasses on, tipped his head back and examined the easel and the frame that was attached to it. With pursed lips, he nodded and went to the table and took a seat. Larry came out of the kitchen carrying the wooden box. He set it on the floor next to the table. Locksmith Lizzie knelt and removed the padlocks. Larry rested a legal pad on the table in front of his chair. He recognized and saluted Helio for being there.

"Thanks. everyone for coming. You all have busy lives, so we're thankful you're a part of the team," Larry said. "Those of you who know me know I like to do things in order—an old army habit—so if you don't mind, I'll steer this ship today."

Everyone nodded in agreement.

"Hi everybody," Sasha said through the Facetime screen. She and Lily Cup waved at the camera.

"Our Paris contingency," Gabe said.

Larry took control.

"First thing we'll do is gather *raison d'etres*—our reasons for being here—each of us will go through what brought us to the table, what we've learned, and what tools we may think we'll need. We'll try to hold off discussion until everyone has presented their case."

Everyone nodded.

"There's no bad information, folks," Larry said. "No wrong answers. We're all in the dark, just trying to shed light on the nightmare friends have found themselves in. We'll go in order. Peck'll go first, then you, Downs, then Chris, then Helio, curator of our art museum."

Ronda raised her hand.

"And you are?" Larry asked.

"Ronda manages a phone store on Canal Street, Larry. She's been good help before, on another case," Peck said.

"Yes, Ronda?" Larry asked.

"Chief Detective Gaines. I'm a sister from the old school. If any of us see a wart—opportunity—can we ask questions or point out the opportunity?"

"You see a wart, Ronda, you shout it out," Larry said.

He pointed at Peck.

Ronda smiled.

"Peck?" Larry asked.

"On Friday, Larry, at Cathedral Basilica a man in a voodoo costume followed me out of church. It was dark. There was a thunderstorm, but no rain. This voodoo man told me he had kidnapped Elizabeth. He didn't use her name—he just said 'her'—but he said if I didn't listen to him, she would die. He put that wooden box in my pickup. He texted me orders. I texted him back. Larry, you told me to always make him prove she's alive. I do every time he texts me and Elizabeth's been leaving—how you say—voice mail messages that she's okay."

"Have you talked to her?" Ronda asked.

"No. He said he'd kill her if I tried. She's leaving clues, though, in the messages she leaves to say she's okay."

"What sort of clues?" Larry asked.

"We think she's in the catacombs under or near the Notre Dame Cathedral, for one. Her guard's name is Elodie for another. It sounds like they're becoming friends. Elizabeth is getting her way a little more every time she leaves clues in my voice mail."

"Anything else, Peck?" Larry asked.

"Ah *oui*. I fly to Paris in two days. I can take one small bag, my passport and the box. I know where I'm supposed to take the box in Paris. He'll give me the code words when I can prove I'm there."

Larry lifted the box from the floor, set it on the table and opened the top and set it back on its hinges.

"Downs?" Larry asked. "You're next."

"Lieutenant, I found the woodworker that made the box in Plaquemine. He didn't put the lining in the box or build any of its interior. He never saw who ordered the box or who picked it up. He was paid in cash, but his wife deposited it in their savings, so no bills are left to check for prints. That's it for me, Lieutenant."

"Where is Plaquemine, Officer Downs?" Chris asked.

"Just as you start into Baton Rouge. It's the first exit."

"Chris, you go next," Larry said.

Chris stood and walked around to the box while pulling a property bag from his pocket. In the bag was the strand of thread he found in the floater's pocket. He held it to the thread on the interior of the box.

"It's a perfect match," he said.

"Folks," Larry said, "a seamstress named Carissa lined this box's interior—velvet and canvas. This piece of thread proves it beyond any doubt. It's a perfect match."

"We found her floating in the canal by Sisters Street, the morning after Bastille Day," Chris added.

"It was murder," Larry said. "We think we can prove the voodoo man drowned her. Motive? She knew too much."

"There's a bigger motive than that, Larry," Peck said.

"What's bigger than that, Peck?"

"She could identify him. That's why she's dead," Peck said.

"I think Peck's right," Lily Cup said.

"I don't understand," Ronda said. "You find someone in the canal and you think it was voodoo man who drowned her? I don't get it. You weren't there. Are you guessing it was him?"

"We have a witness who saw her board a boat we think he was on. We found a rubber snake tied around her waist that wasn't on her when she boarded," Larry said.

"Oh, so sorry, Chief Detective," Ronda said.

"The man on the boat had makeup on his chin, and the voodoo man who threatened Peck carried a long rubber snake on his arm," Larry said.

"Peck, can I ask you something?" Ronda asked.

"Ah *oui*. *A*x me anything, Ronda."

"This Elodie bitch—the one guarding Elizabeth in the catacombs?"

"Ah *oui*?"

"If she's guarding a kidnappee—is that the right word?—and they're talking to each other, I think this sister is either not connected personally to this voodoo man, or she's not too smart."

"Right," Peck said.

"Where are you going with this?" Larry asked.

"Chief Detective," Ronda said. "If Elodie is this loose-lipped now, after a couple days, but she's still staying the course with Elizabeth—sounds to me she's nervous and scared."

"What are you saying?" Larry asked.

"Larry," Lily Cup said, "what Ronda's saying is Elodie, that guard, is dumber than dog shit and the minute this is over, she probably knows she'll be dead, too, just like the seamstress."

"Peck, what's your take?" Larry asked.

Helio stood with a file folder in his hand.

"Chief Detective, before Peck answers, might I put a word in?" Helio asked.

"Be our guest, Helio."

"Thank you, Chief Detective."

Helio walked to the artist's easel.

"People," he said, "I want you to look at these dark shreds. They are fibers of canvas hanging on the inside edge of this frame mounted behind the outer heavy gold frame."

He lifted an eight-by-ten photo of a painting from his file folder and held it up.

"This is a picture of a world-famous painting, *The Storm on the Sea of Galilee,* by Rembrandt. The canvas cut out of this frame was a copy of the original painting."

"How is this relevant to Elizabeth's kidnapping, Helio?" Larry asked.

"Chief Detective," Helio said. "*The Storm on the Sea of Galilee* is priceless—one of the most valuable paintings in the world."

"And …?" Larry asked.

"These shreds of canvas on this giclee of that master are clues, Chief Lieutenant," Helio said.

"Go on," Larry said.

"The giclee painting that was cut from this frame is only worth the value of the frame and the few dollars it cost to print it—" Helio started.

"What am I missing, Helio?" Larry asked. "What clues?"

"Chief Detective, the original of this painting, *The Storm on the Sea of Galilee,* was cut from its frame with a blade in this exact same fashion when it was stolen. The Isabella Stewart Gardner Museum in Boston was robbed of the original Rembrandt in the biggest art robbery in history—over three hundred million dollars in paintings stolen in that one heist. The thieves cut the painting out of the frame with a razor blade of some sort and left threads of canvas, just like these."

"Hot dang!" Gabe yelped.

"Peck—do you know why he's making you go to Paris?" Ronda asked.

"I'm taking the box, giving it to somebody...."

"That makes you the voodoo's mule," Chris said.

"Ah *oui*."

"But why Peck?" Larry asked. "Why's he the mule?"

"We need to know what's in the box," Lily Cup said.

"We're afraid to look—in case it's a trap," Larry said.

"Chief Detective," Ronda replied, "excuse my French, but I have to agree with Lily Cup in Paris. Whoever is behind this has to be dumber than rat shit—that's a given, what with a talkative guard in the catacombs. But that doesn't make this evil man not a survivor. Most scum like this aren't stupid about their own survival," Ronda said.

"Ideas anyone?" Larry asked.

No one responded.

"Locksmith Lizzie, what's your forensic take on all this?" Larry asked.

"I agree with Ronda and Lily Cup, Lieutenant."

"Fuck it, then. Let's see what's in the box," Larry said.

Lily Cup applauded from Paris. Ronda and Aurelie joined her. Lizzie stepped over to the box, prepared to get into it.

"Chief Detective," Ronda said. "Before Lizzie empties the box, can I try something I learned in a psych class in college?"

"Go for it," Larry said.

"Peck, you told us Elizabeth calls your phone from her phone and leaves you voice mail messages."

"Ah *oui*."

"And you told us you're not allowed to talk to her or to send her messages?" Ronda asked.

"That's right."

"How do you make contact with her?"

"I text the voodoo man. He tells the guard somehow—I guess by text—to tell Elizabeth to leave a voice mail for me."

"Why would he do that, do your bidding like that, contacting Elizabeth—like he was at your beck and call?" Ronda asked.

"Cause if he sends me messages, I always tell him to prove she's alive, first. That's when he does it."

"Got it! What's the phone number that calls you?"

"Hanh?" Peck asked.

"What's on your mind, Ronda?" Larry asked.

"Chief Detective, nobody told Peck Sasha or Lily Cup couldn't contact her," Ronda said. "Give them her phone number, Peck. I'd like to see what number calls you."

Peck pointed to Larry for approval. Larry nodded.

"Go ahead, give Lily Cup the number, Peck."

"Lily Cup, will you text Peck your number, please? I want to call you," Ronda said.

"Sure," Lily Cup said.

"Thank you, Chief Detective. Carry on, ladies and gentlemen. Don't mind me. I'm going to step over to a corner and call Lily Cup and come up with a plan. I believe you were about to search the box?" Ronda asked.

Chapter 27

While the others took a bathroom break, Lizzie emptied the box.

"Folks," Larry declared, "everything from inside the box is out on the table, including the giclee print, *The Storm on the Sea of Galilee.* Good job, Lizzie."

"Thank you, Lieutenant."

"Nancy Kirkwood printed the giclee and was murdered because she could have identified the voodoo man," Chris said. "Just as the seamstress was murdered because she knew his face."

"Exactly," Larry said. "You can put it all back in the box, Lizzie."

Helio, from the museum, stood.

"Fourteen framed *Stations of the Cross*—total value maybe seven-hundred dollars at best," Helio said. "One rolled up giclee of *The Storm on the Sea of Galilee,* worth maybe seventy-five dollars retail."

"What's your point, Helio?" Larry asked.

"This is hardly worth murdering two people for, Chief Detective."

"Helio, you're saying the rolled-up canvas is the same as a stolen famous painting," Peck said.

"I am."

"Doesn't that make it—how you say—a forgery?" Peck asked.

"If it's sold as a giclee print, it isn't a forgery, Peck— merely a print. But if it's sold as an original, it would be a forgery," Helio said. "I believe the *Stations of the Cross* prints are a ruse to get through Customs, but my guess is the prize is the forgery some collector of stolen art will pay for."

"There's nothing in this box that would cause suspicion or stop it from getting through Customs leaving the US or crossing into France," Larry said.

He looked at Peck. "Peck, it's time you do your thing."

Peck got up and began rambling.

"The Notre Dame Cathedral caught on fire and burned. And within a week people from all over the world donated billions of dollars to rebuild it. That's a lot of money, and that's a lot of rich people going to Paris to write checks and watch.

"I think the voodoo man is selling this giclee forgery as an original painting—the famous stolen painting, Helio has told us about—to someone rich for a lot of money.

"I'm thinking the voodoo man called the Notre Dame Cathedral and told them that if he could sell a valuable painting he would donate the money to them—which was a scam—and maybe they put a rich art collector in touch with him. And now he's going to sell him a fake.

"And I'm his mule."

"Why you as the mule, Peck? What do you think he's up to?" Larry asked.

"If a rich guy isn't too smart, Larry, he's sure to have smart people around him, figuring things out, protecting him. The voodoo man's making me the mule because if the man or woman buying it finds out it's a forgery after they paid millions for it, I'd be the one who gets killed, not the voodoo man."

"Arrested maybe, but why would they have you killed, Peck?" Aurelia asked.

"This is a stolen art, bébé. If they reported it to the police, they would be arrested for trying to buy it. They're crooks if they're buying stolen art."

"And with no living witnesses alive to identify him, the voodoo man could run, hide and try something else—another con."

Ronda raised her hand.

"Go ahead, Ronda," Larry said.

"Lily Cup, Sasha?" Ronda asked.

"We hear you loud and clear."

"Anything to report?"

"$25,000 US," Lily Cup said. "She said she would let her go for $25,000 US."

"Ladies, what's going on?" Larry asked.

Lily Cup held her phone to Sasha's for Larry to see the text.

"I don't understand," Larry said.

"Chief Detective, Lily Cup just convinced Elodie she could get her $25,000 if she would let Elizabeth go," Ronda said.

"It looks real," Larry said. "Peck, you look at it."

"Read it to me, Lily Cup," Peck said.

"Peck, it says $25,000 will light the candle," Lily Cup said.

"That is real, Larry," Peck said.

"It could be a trap, Peck."

"It's real, Larry, because the text says '$25,000 will *light the candle,*'" Peck said.

"Is that supposed to mean something?" Larry asked.

"It's Elizabeth's code to me, always. When the coast was clear she'd light a candle I could see through her window," Peck said. "If all was good and I could come in the house, there was a candle lit on the mantle. If the coast wasn't clear, there was no candle lit. Elizabeth sent this text, I'm sure. It's for real."

"Lily Cup, Sasha—listen up," Larry said.

"We're here," Lily Cup said.

"Talk to them, Ronda," Larry said.

"Lily Cup, did Elodie text you detail?" Ronda asked.

"In exactly three hours, a black car will be pulling up in front of the Lafayette Museum in Paris—9 Rue du Platre," Lily Cup said.

"I know that museum," Sasha said.

"A limousine?" Ronda asked.

"It'll be a small, black Fiat with tape over its license plates. It will pull up. We'll be able to read *Netherland* on the plates," Lily Cup said.

"Why three hours?" Larry asked.

"She texted me that she has her boyfriend's car keys and she has to go get the car and come back to where she was holding Elizabeth," Lily Cup said.

"Black, Fiat, Netherland," Ronda said. "Got it."

"Elizabeth will be in that black Fiat. I'll spread the cash out like a fan and with a firm grip hold it out for the driver—let her grab hold of it, too, until Elizabeth is out of the car. Once she's out, I'll release the hold on the cash," Lily Cup said.

"Got it," Ronda said.

"If you don't have the cash in your hand when she drives up, she'll drive away and disappear in traffic with Elizabeth, back to the catacombs," Peck said.

"I understand," Lily Cup said.

"Lily Cup, does Elodie think a man or a woman will have the cash in hand?" Larry asked.

"She thinks it'll be a woman."

"We've got to think fast, ladies," Larry said. "There's no time to waste. Sasha, you go get the cash. Lily Cup, you get to the nearest police station and call me from there immediately. We'll get an undercover police woman to make the trade. Elizabeth will probably be handcuffed. The police woman will have a key. Will the museum still be open in three hours?"

"It'll be open," Sasha said. "Won't she arrest the woman for kidnapping?" Lily Cup asked.

"Not to worry," Larry said. "I'll call the Paris police. I'll clue them in. They will know this is the beginning of a Paris sting operation to entrap and to catch a multiple murderer. They'll know the woman is just a pawn and will let her leave the country with the money—but not let her return."

"Okay," Sasha said.

"Sasha, Lily Cup—this is Chris."

"We can hear you, Chris."

"You two get inside the museum, out of sight and wait for Elizabeth in there. We'll see to it the lady officer takes her inside to you. Put a scarf on her head and get her to your hotel. Don't let her leave your room until we tell you."

"Got it," Lily Cup said.

"I'll repay every cent, beautiful ladies," Gabe shouted.

"Lily Cup, this is Peck. You need a code."

"What do you mean?" Sasha asked.

"To make sure it's Elizabeth. The lady officer never met her."

"That's right. What sort of code?" Lily Cup asked.

"Ask her, 'what's Peck's name?'"

"Perfect. The answer is?"

"Boudreaux Clemont Finch," Peck said.

"Got it. We've got to go," Lily Cup said.

They clicked off Facetime.

"What now, Larry?" Peck asked. "Do I go or stay?"

"Let's play this out first—see how it goes," Larry said.

"Lieutenant, if Peck is the mule going to Paris for the voodoo man, isn't it reasonable to think the voodoo man will keep clear of Paris and stay here in New Orleans until the con happens and the money for the forgery hits his bank account?" Chris asked.

"I'd bet on it," Larry said.

"Then why don't we let Peck go to Paris with the box—play it out? But we'll see that he gets followed by undercover Paris police backup. We foil the forgery sting and trace the money to the voodoo man and catch him here for murder and kidnapping while he's still here, in the states," Chris said.

"Peck?" Larry asked.

"He's right, Larry. I'll go," Peck said.

Gabe stood up.

"My military training tells me we should look at our end game, folks—our tactics and strategy," Gabe said. "We want to catch a murderer."

"That's it—the end game," Larry said.

"Larry, if the buyer of the forgery Peck delivers it to gets arrested, the voodoo man will evaporate into thin air. Larry, you've got to convince the Paris police backup not to arrest the buyer."

"There's no crime in buying an eighty-dollar giclee print," Helio said.

"There is if he thinks he's buying a stolen piece of art," Larry said. "That's misprision of a felony."

"What does it all mean?" Chris asked.

"He's not buying a stolen original. He's buying a forgery. He can't be arrested for being stupid," Helio said.

"If an accused has knowledge of a crime and he does not reveal it to the right authorities it is misprision. The law could make a case he knew he was buying stolen art—which would also make him an accessory to two murders that we know of," Larry said.

"There's something you might consider, Lieutenant—between France and the US," Chris said.

"I'm listening," Larry said.

"If you do catch the voodoo man here in New Orleans for murder, Chief Detective, you'll eliminate any problem of trying to get him out of France," Chris said.

"How's that?" Gabe asked.

"France won't extradite a prisoner—even on murder—if the penalty for the crime here is death. We still do the needle," Chris said.

"So, if the sting will be the catching of the voodoo man—we let the forgery sale go through?" Peck asked.

"Let me think on that," Larry said. "Might be I'll get Paris to let the 'sale' go through and the money transferred just to smoke the voodoo man out of hiding. On the condition the buyer agrees to cooperate, we'll snatch the voodoo man the minute he tries to collect the money," Larry said. "The buyer may get his money back, and we'll give the voodoo man a free ride to Angola. But this is all speculation. Let's see how the Elizabeth release goes first."

"I'll text Lily Cup. I'll tell her to make sure Elodie keeps her phone and answering texts from the voodoo man, just like they're still in the catacombs," Peck said.

"That's good detective work, Peck," Larry said.

"Tell her it's for both their safety until this is over."

"I've done it," Peck said. "I already got a smile emoticon texted back."

"I'm off to see the mayor," Charlie said.

"What's on your mind, Charlie?" Larry asked.

"Latoya Cantrell is an acquaintance of the president of France. I'm going to see if she can pull some strings for us in Paris."

Chapter 28

"Good morning, sir, how can I help you?" a receptionist asked.

"Is Mayor Cantrell in?" Charlie asked.

"And you are?"

"The name's Charlie—a barkeep from Frenchman Street."

"May I ask what business you have with the mayor?"

Charlie gave a brief synopsis of what was happening in New Orleans and in Paris. The receptionist asked him to wait and went in the office behind her. When she came out, she handed Charlie a business card.

"Sir, Mayor Cantrell is preparing to meet with the city council. Then the mayor will attend a luncheon at Tulane. She asked me to give you her card. Please email the mayor with as much detail as you can how you think she can help. If the mayor has any questions, someone will get back to you late today," the receptionist said.

"Thank you," Charlie said.

"As much detail as you can provide in your email."

"Yes, ma'am."

Charlie left the mayor's offices.

Peck was with Gabe at the Columns Hotel having shrimp and grits when his iPhone rang. It was a Paris phone number. He sat up straight—showed the phone to Gabe and answered it.

"Hello?"

"Peck—it's me."

"Elizabeth, for real?"

"*Oui*. I'm safe," Elizabeth said.

"Cher—just to hear your voice."

"Tu ne peux pas imaginer à quel point je voulais entendre ta voix, Peck. J'avais peur de ne plus jamais te revoir." ("You can't imagine how much I wanted to hear your voice, Peck. I was scared I would never see you again.")

"Vous ont-ils blessé?" ("Did they hurt you?")

"I was freezing cold all the time, but I'm okay. Elodie is out of the country by now, or well on her way, I think. They told her she'd never be allowed back in France."

"Does she know your name?" Peck asked.

"She thinks my name is Millie. I never corrected her."

"Millie?"

"Yes, isn't that curious?"

"Ah *oui*. Was there a man?"

"At the airport, there was a man with Elodie. The man had a picture of me in his hand, but I couldn't see it when they approached me. He tried to hide it in his pocket. That's when I saw it."

"Could you see his face?"

"I will never forget that face."

"Are you with Lily Cup and Sasha?"

"I'm at a police station."

"What?"

"Don't worry. I'm okay. They didn't want Lily Cup and Sasha to be seen with me in case anyone was watching or following. They wanted to ask me questions. I told them everything I know, which wasn't much."

"Cher, did Elodie tell you why she did it—who was behind it?"

"C'était sommaire, mais elle l'a fait." ("It was sketchy, but she did.")

"Comment l'as-tu fait parler, cher?" ("How did you get her to talk? In English, cher. My frien' Gabe is listening too."

"Ah *oui*. One night Elodie had tears in her eyes, and I asked her what was wrong. She told me and that's when she started talking."

"Ah *oui*. I figured somehow you got close to her."

"She told me she was with a lover on the Left Bank—they were kissing. A man with a scarf around his face grabbed her lover's collar from behind and put a gun to his head and told Elodie if she didn't do what he told her to do—and get in his van—he would shoot her lover. She got in his van and watched him stick a needle in her lover's neck and leave him on the bench. That's why Elodie pretended to be all smiles and grabbed me after I got through customs. She came up alone like she was a sister or a friend or something and hugged me, making it look like I knew her. At first, I thought she was someone from the bistro where I'll be chef coming to give me a ride."

"Cher, I was confused with one of your messages that Elodie asked you if you liked caviar. Why did she ask you that? Do you know?"

"Ah *oui,* Peck. She told me you would know who to give the box to when someone approached you and offered you a jar of caviar. That would be the signal that you were to give it to him."

"Did they kill her lover, cher?"

"Elodie said the man told her the needle he stuck in her lover's neck would only make him sleep, but when she drove me to the museum Lafayette, she told me she didn't know if he was alive or dead but because his car was still in the same parking place, he was probably dead. The man who stuck the needle in him took her phone and threw it and the needle in the Seine and then gave her a phone and ordered her to use it. She was afraid to call her lover on that phone."

"That was lucky for you—her not trying to call him."

"The police lady told me you're coming to Paris—"

"Cher, get some sleep. We'll talk later."

"I'm so tired."

"I'll tell you everything when you wake up."

"The police are taking me where your friends are."

"They're your friends, too, cher."

"I'll get to sleep warm for the first time in Paris."

Peck thought it best not to go deeper into dialogue of his coming to Paris. He ended the call with a promise to talk soon.

"I'll bet that call, my brother, just lifted a ton off your shoulders," Gabe said.

"Did you hear the clue in the call, ol' man?"

"Don't tell me she was talking in code, son?"

"Nah-nah, but they thought her name was Millie."

"Where's that take you, Peck?"

"It means the voodoo man's been spying on me—here in New Orleans. I have to figure out where he's been spying."

"Things are in three's here in our pelican city, my brother, don't forget that."

"Ah *oui*."

"Our shotgun house, Charlie's Blue Note, and the Cathedral Basilica—that's your three, son. The answer's in there somewhere."

"Ah *oui*."

Chapter 29

"Gabe, order another beer. I'm still hungry. I have to make a call. I'll be right back," Peck said.

"Where're you going, son?" Gabe asked.

"Across the lobby into the—how you say—parlor, Gabe. No one's over there and I can make a call without ears."

"My brother, you're tracking again. Go. Beer and another meal will be waiting when you get back."

In the Column Hotel's parlor Peck Facetime-called Father McBride from Cathedral Basilica. When he answered, Father McBride was standing by a window with a cup of coffee in his hand.

"Peck, such a pleasure. To what do I owe the honor of this visit with my favorite fan of the Basilica?" Father McBride asked.

"Father McBride, do you have an office where you can go while we talk—in private?"

"I'm in my office, Peck. Let me sit at my desk."

Father McBride moved the iPhone image around dizzily until resting it on his desk in front of him. He sat down, smiled and waved at Peck.

"Father McBride—there's been trouble."

Father McBride sat erect, giving his full attention.

"Father McBride, you can't talk with anyone about what I'm going to tell you—do you understand?"

"I understand, Peck, but I am responsible to the archbishop. I—"

"Not even the archbishop, bishop, Pope, nobody, Father McBride. You have to trust me on this."

"You have my word—I will follow your guidance."

"And ask me no questions."

"Oh my. Should I be frightened, Peck?"

"Father, there's a chance that someone bugged me in your confessional. There is a chance that a vicious stalker who has already killed two people has been listening in on my confessions."

Father McBride was stunned into silence.

"I'm going to have a lady from the police go over and check the cathedral and the confessional for bugs, Father McBride. Her name is Lizzie. She will have identification from NOLA forensics. I'll see she calls you first."

"I'm stunned, Peck. But I trust your instincts implicitly."

"Thank you, Father."

"May I ask if you are in any way—in harm's way, Peck?"

"Don't ask, Father, but pray, please."

"I will have a Mass said for you, my son."

"Thank you, Father. Can I ax you something, Father?'

"Of course."

"On the wall behind you—what is that hanging on those two hooks, like a hat rack thing?"

Father McBride turned to look up at the wall.

"Oh those," he said. "Some beads from a parade or two, my knit cap from my Bastille Day costume—"

"The rosary beads, Father McBride. Those big, oversize, long rosary beads, Father?"

Father McBride started to reach for the rosary beads hanging on the hook.

"Oh these ...."

"Don't touch them," Peck said.

Father McBride froze.

"Father, don't touch those rosary beads. Can you remember when and where you got them?"

"I remember exactly, Peck. I was coming back to the rectory following the Bastille Day festivities, and I found them in the parking lot just behind my car. A reveler must have dropped them."

"Father McBride, do you remember Larry?"

"Chief Detective Larry—certainly I remember the man."

"Father, someone will be coming over there to take those rosary beads. If they show proper identification, let them take them. Don't touch them, Father. They'll know how to lift them down."

"Checking them for fingerprints, are you, Peck?"

"Ah *oui*, Father."

"Oh, dear—and in my parking space."

"Father, of all my friens' I told you about—and my lady friens'—do you remember the names of any of the girls?"

"Oh my—you have so many friends, so many stories you've shared. I would say Millie is the love of your life. Are you still with Millie, Peck? Has she moved to the city?"

"Father, I have to go now. I'll call you soon."

"You're in my prayers, Boudreaux—please be safe."

Peck clicked off and called Larry.

"Talk to me," Larry said.

Peck told him about the opportunity for prints on the rosary beads and the possible bug in the confessional that Locksmith Lizzie should check out.

"What triggered this, Peck?"

"Elizabeth called me—from a police station in Paris."

"Is she okay? What'd she say?"

"She's okay—said whoever kidnapped her thought her name was Millie—kept calling her Millie. Larry, the only place where anyone could know about Millie or relate me with her would be at Charlie's Blue Note or, I'm thinking, in the confessional when I go."

"He's a stalker, you think? Planted a bug, maybe?"

"Larry, can you send Lizzie to the cathedral to check?"

"Right away. What else, Peck?"

"Have her ask for Father McBride."

"Check."

"Larry, on Father McBride's wall behind his desk there are giant rosary beads he found in the parking lot on Bastille Day."

While Peck was on the phone, Larry pressed his shortwave.

"Headquarters, this is unit nine-eight-four calling headquarters. Come back."

"This is headquarters, Unit nine-eight-four."

"Headquarters I need Officer Downs at the Cathedral Basilica rectory—ask for Father McBride."

There was a slight pause.

"Unit nine-eight-four—Officer Downs is on his way."

"Headquarters, instruct Officer Downs to have the rosary beads checked for prints urgently. Do you copy? Urgently."

"Unit nine-eight-four, this is Officer Downs. I'm on it. Over and out."

"Larry, I think I still have to go to Paris," Peck said.

"It's looking good about all the players being here, Peck. What's on your mind about Paris?" Larry asked.

"One of the clues, Larry—the Elodie woman told Elizabeth about some kind of boat—*De Peniche a Paris*. I think the voodoo man lives on it on that river in Paris."

"The Seine?" Larry asked.

"Ah *oui,* that's it," Peck said. "I think he lives there."

"Let's wait it out, Peck. I know it'll be rough, but after we get a read from our visits to the Basilica, we'll know which way to turn."

"Okay. Call me if you hear anything, frien'."

Peck rejoined Gabe, drank beer and ate Cajun fare.

Chapter 30

Peck was asleep in his room at the shotgun. The night, its sounds of loneliness crawling through the city once again. His bedroom door opened slowly and then closed behind a female form spotlighted by a streetlamp through open shades of the window. The woman pulled her hair back into a pony tail. Peck opened his eyes enough to peek. It was Aurelie.

"Ton ami Gabe m'a laissé entrer. Es-tu fou ?" Aurelie asked. ("Your friend Gabe let me in. Are you mad?")

Peck didn't answer.

She slowly unbuttoned an ivory silk blouse, her eyes glued to Peck's eyes as he watched her fingers. She removed the blouse. She wore no bra. She unbuttoned her skirt waist, and it dropped to the floor. She lifted a leg and rested her foot on the bed. She leaned forward to unbuckle the shoe, and the streetlamp on her supple breasts cast their shadows on a tight, firm stomach. Peck reached to the side table for protection, rolled on his back, put it on and pulled the sheet away. Aurelie never made a sound. Her eyes spoke for her. She crawled on the bed, pulled his briefs down to his knees, straddled him and, holding his cheeks, kissed and sucked his lips while sensuously grinding her hips and love island on his warmth until a throbbing William found the way and pushed in to begin their journey to a third shivering ecstasy—something they needed from each other after working so closely, so tirelessly. The moment came, again and again—and then they were one.

They were resting but connected when Peck's phone rang. It was Larry. Aurelie reached for the phone and handed it to Peck.

"Larry?" Peck asked.

"That was some stellar police work, my friend—you spotting those rosary beads like that," Larry said.

"They're his?" Peck asked.

"Peck, my friend, how would you like to do the honors tonight?" Larry quipped.

"*Aye yi-yi*!" Peck said. "Talk to me, frien'!"

"His name is Frederick Bolton. He's a small-time con man—a hood. He has arrest warrants for petty theft in three states. He's a starving artist, an oil painter. He rarely sells anything and lives on a—"

"Don't tell me, frien'. He lives on a *péniche* in Paris—a houseboat on that Seine River?"

Larry laughed. "Ready for this, Peck?"

"Ah *oui*."

"Our friend Frederick Bolton just happens to live at a marina on a cruiser named—ready?"

"Ah *oui*."

"A cruiser named *Le Péniche à Paris*. That's the name of his boat, Peck. There's no houseboat in Paris. He's on *Le Péniche à Paris*, a cruiser in a slip right here at the marina on Lake Borgne, right now."

"What's the plan, Larry?"

"Tide's out, Peck. It's going to be pretty smelly down there—washed up baitfish and silt."

"Larry, I grew up with those smells, frien'. What's the plan?"

"Listen good," Larry said.

"Ah *oui*."

"First thing is—if this all goes down as we hope tonight—tomorrow we're going to overnight the box to the Paris police. They'll have an undercover officer meet up with the buyer of the stolen art."

"That'll work, Larry. But remember, I'll need a picture of the Notre Dame taken from the bridge—like I took it? I'll have to send it to the voodoo man."

"That's already being done, Peck. You'll be getting pictures soon. Lily Cup is waiting for dark and will take a few from that bridge and send them to you."

"That's smart thinking, Larry—good idea. He'll think I'm in Paris."

"Exactly, son—a good sting."

"Larry, tell the police the code to know the buyer is the guy who will come on the bridge and offer him a jar of caviar."

"Sounds like a plan, Peck."

"Will they arrest him, Larry?"

"I'm sure they'll have plenty of volunteers pressing charges on his conduct, Peck, so my guess is yes—but only if we pull off this grab tonight. They'll let us play it out first. Are you up to the task, Peck?"

"I'm up to it. I'm ready, Larry."

"I'll have the marina docks surrounded by an undercover team with one sharpshooter. I'll text you the dock number and the boat name, so you can make a visual. Don't drive there, Peck. He knows your pickup. You need to take an Uber to the address I send you."

"Larry, I don't know the Uber—"

"I do," Aurelie whispered.

Peck touched the speaker button.

"Never mind, Larry, my mistake. I do know Uber—sorry. When do I go?"

"Listen carefully, Peck," Larry said.

"Ah *oui*."

"Can you get a woman's stocking to put over your head?"

Aurelie sat up on William and began rolling one of her stockings down her leg.

"I got one, Larry," Peck said.

"Peck, we'll have an expansion microphone—like a bionic ear on a nearby boat recording every word you and the voodoo man say. As you get near his boat, Peck, pull the stocking over your head … the plan is if he doesn't recognize you, you'll be able to buy more time and get him to blab, get him to admit some things we can use as evidence."

"I get it, Larry. I set the hooks, bait the trap?"

"You got it, my friend. Make up any bullshit you want to make him come out—you know how."

"Won't he know it's me, Larry? Even with the stocking mask?"

"He may think it, but if he's as dumb as it's looking, he'll have his doubts. Just don't let him play you. You play him."

"Ah *oui*."

"And one more thing," Larry said.

"What?"

"Peck, we know what this bastard has done to you, to your friend, and those now in graves. My team's going to turn a blind eye, Peck, when you board his boat, but whatever you do, don't kill him. As much as you'll want to—don't do it."

"Ah *oui*."

"Give me your word, son," Larry said. "I won't be able to save you this time."

"You've got my word, Larry."

"Look for my texts, Peck, but when you get on the dock remember to turn your phone off so he can't sucker entrap you by calling your number. See you soon."

Larry clicked off. Peck looked up at Aurelie, sitting on him.

"William's still ready, Peck. Want to do it again?"

Peck lifted Aurelie off, removed the protection, stood up, and took a towel from the dresser.

"I've got to go—catch the voodoo man, bébé."

Aurelie squatted cross-legged on the bed and handed the stocking to him. She grabbed William.

"Let me come with you?"

"It's too dangerous, bébé."

Aurelie gently stroked William.

"If you Uber, I'll have to go. It's my account. I'm going."

"On one condition, bébé."

"What condition?"

"When we get there, you sit on a bench someplace and don't move a muscle until it's over."

"I promise."

"Okay."

"So, I can go?" Aurelie squealed.

"Ah *oui*."

She kissed William.

"Peck, after it's over you'll need Uber back here and—"

"So you'll come home with me tonight, bébé."

Chapter 31

Peck was dressed in black jeans and T-shirt when Larry's phone texted him a marina name and address and dock number and boat slip ID.

Peck stuffed the red stocking in his pocket. He sat on the bed and began studying a map on his phone as if he were studying times and distances and escape routes from the marina. Aurelie took her garter belt and the other stocking off and put them in her carryall bag. She pulled shorts and sneakers from the bag and put them on. She stepped over to Peck bare-chested, held the back of his head and pulled his face into her breast.

"Can I borrow a T-shirt?" she asked.

Peck smiled, licked her nipple and pointed at the second drawer down on his dresser. Gabe was asleep in his room when they made their way outside. An Uber SUV pulled up.

"Go get in, bébé. I'll be right with you."

As Aurelie climbed into the SUV, Peck reached in under the seat of his pickup and brought out a bronze cane—one he left there for defense, should he ever need it. He climbed in and they drove off.

The city was always lonely at night. Poverty kept no hours.

At the marina were two benches on either side of the wood entryway dock. Four fishermen were waiting for the incoming tide, when flounder come in to feed on the bait shrimp. A man with a paper-bagged bourbon bottle cradled in his arms was asleep on one of the benches.

"Wait here, bébé," Peck told Aurelie.

He stepped over to a husky black man sitting on a bench, balancing two fishing rods between his legs, a small ice chest to his side.

"Mister, you've got a good face," Peck said.

The man looked up and smiled.

"Peck Finch?" the man whispered.

"Ah *oui*—how did you—?"

The man opened his wallet, showed his badge, then closed it rapidly.

"Your friend will be safe with me," the man said.

"Is Larry—?" Peck started.

"He's on a boat behind the target, but in view. Time to go do your magic, son. Good luck. We've got your back."

Peck motioned for Aurelie to sit on the bench. The plainclothes man held out a beer for her. Peck gripped his bronze cane and walked in a quick pace, evolving his psyche from prey to predator.

There was a tall, wooded pier lamp pole towering over the walking deck ramp. The cruiser, *Le Péniche à Paris*, was docked there. A man was standing on the aft deck in front of an easel, painting under the light of the harbor streetlamp. The image he was painting was of a large yacht anchored fifty feet away. Peck clutched the stocking, pulled it over his head and jumped on board. Without the voodoo man even taking notice, he stepped onto the aft deck, holding his bronze cane in alert.

"Millie's dead," Peck growled.

"I don't know what you're talking about, *Monsieur*. Please get off my boat."

"The girl's dead, too," Peck said.

The voodoo man set his paintbrush down and lifted his cell phone. He texted a message to Elodie. Just as Lily Cup had instructed her, Elodie, now safe at home in the Netherlands, answered the text as though she were still in the catacombs under Notre Dame.

The voodoo man held up his phone for Peck to see. He smirked at Peck.

"I'm afraid this one will do anything I tell her to do, *Monsieur.*"

"You're a fool, *Monsieur.* You wouldn't know how to murder. You're a shoplifter, a scam artist."

"I'll not waste my time, skipping into your traps of words, *Monsieur.* I'm a serious painter. I am building a catalogue of great sailing vessels," the voodoo man said.

"Like *The Storm on the Sea of Galilee, Monsieur?*" Peck asked.

The voodoo man froze.

"What do you know of this, as you say, *The Storm on the Sea of Galilee?*"

"I know that person who will be standing near the Notre Dame Cathedral the day after tomorrow will not be receiving the painting until, shall we say, we create a partnership?"

"I don't know what you're talking about. I'm just a painter."

"Okay, my mistake. *Bon soir, Monsieur,*" Peck said. He turned to step off the boat.

"No, wait," the voodoo man said.

Peck paused.

As the voodoo man began to speak, Peck watched him secretly grabbing a hypodermic needle from the easel and clutching it in his palm.

"Are you wearing a wire, *Monsieur?*" the voodoo man asked.

Peck lifted his T-shirt, showing a bare midriff.

"*Monsieur,* perhaps if you don't get in the way of the Notre Dame appointment, would you consider half a million as a good and fair partnership?"

"Hmm," Peck said. "Half a million? It's a very valuable painting. I don't know."

"A million," the voodoo man said.

"A million would do it, *Monsieur.* But the two girls will have to be taken care of, and I don't do that sort of thing," Peck said.

"I'll take care of them—don't worry. You'll get a million to not interfere with the transfer, and I'll see that those two girls disappear," the voodoo man said.

"But you're an artist, *Monsieur*. What do you know about making people disappear?" Peck asked.

"I'm quite talented. I've made a lady disappear in a nearby canal. I made a lady vanish from a studio on Magazine Street. I made the lover of that pretty little girl in the catacombs disappear into the Left Bank," the voodoo man said.

"I get one million, and you'll clean up the eyes and ears, *Monsieur*?" Peck asked.

"Shall we shake on it, *Monsieur*?" the voodoo man asked.

He extended his right hand for a shake. Peck reached and grabbed the man's wrist on the hand holding the needle. He raised the bronze can to strike a blow.

"No, no, *Monsieur*, not my painting hand—I beg you."

"Drop the needle and I won't," Peck said.

The voodoo man dropped the needle on the deck, and Peck crushed it with his shoe. Peck flattened the voodoo man's arm and maneuvered the hand to a gunnel.

"Grab the gunnel," Peck said.

The voodoo man clutched the gunnel with his hand. With lightning speed Peck glanced three bone crushing clunks with the bronze cane on the voodoo man's knuckles, shattering them. The voodoo man was screaming in pain as three armed officers jumped on the deck.

"We've got it all on tape. We'll take it from here."

"You said you wouldn't hurt my painting hand, *Monsieur!*"

"Only a fool would have believed me," Peck said.

www.ingramcontent.com/pod-product-compliance
Lightning Source LLC
Chambersburg PA
CBHW051828020726
47502CB00005B/1686